Slices

Also by Laurie Brady and published by Ginninderra Press

Rummy

Rapport

Laurie Brady

Slices

Slices
ISBN 978 1 76041 409 2
Copyright © Laurie Brady 2017
Cover: People in confusion. Concept of fusion
of thoughts © puckillustrations

First published 2017 by
GINNINDERRA PRESS
PO Box 3461 Port Adelaide 5015
www.ginninderrapress.com.au

Contents

Memories

Memory isn't always an act of will. It often creeps up and surprises us, slips through our defences. That's why I wanted to see her again after all these years, now an old lady, a widow rattling around in her half empty house with mementos of a receding past, and clocks that tick too loud.

Opening the old rusty gate was a time warp, re-entering the distant past. Even the doorbell saddened me, a choking sound as if it too had been infected by the years. She stood nonplussed for a few seconds, blinking in the light, before delight spread across her face, and I was greeted like the long lost son.

Little had changed in the sitting room. The same old teak buffet, the same floral lounge, though the arms were judiciously covered with offcuts of velvet, no doubt to cover the wear, and the same table where I used to sit and play rummy with the family, and where I was now ushered for the obligatory cup of tea.

'I've been thinking a lot about David recently,' I told her. 'The past seems to gather a sweetness in the memory,' I felt the need to say. 'Even things that were once painful eventually stop hurting.' I wondered if I'd said too much.

Waiting for the kettle to boil, she placed her hand affectionately on my shoulder and smiled enigmatically, a smile that seemed to carry acceptance more than wistfulness. 'I have so few,' she remarked, referring to the six photos she brought with the tea, and spread out in a row on the table.

*

The first was a black and white Brownie box camera snap that showed David in his overalls, strapped up so tight they jacked his groin. At nine, his ears are sticking out, and the early moment of his 'cheese' has caught him with a foolish look. In the background, the old garage sheds skin, and paspalum licks the paling fence. On the ground in front of him are birthday gifts, a dartboard, a plastic truck, some bags of sweets and, to the right, the bushy tail of the family dog, no doubt shooed away too late and therefore partly immortalised.

David and I met on our first day at school. I can even remember standing next to him with our mothers, and the teachers showering us with what must have been dulcet words, sing-song asking our names and patting our heads that we turned to hide on our mother's hips. Our mothers were blinking their tearful eyes, and laughing at their silliness, as we were led into our classrooms, all milky-white innocence.

In those infant years, we sat next to each other in class, and in the playground we were inseparable, often as a galloping horse, with one of us at the front and the other at the rear, chasing the other children. 'And why was I always the horse's rump?' he'd laughingly joke in our adult years. Not that he always was.

As childhood friends and neighbours, we'd often play in the cubby house, a wooden packing case for cars my father had purchased for a few dollars, and disembowelled behind the privet in our backyard. They were balmy afternoon eternities when time was never harried, and we ventured in our spaceship submarine that braved every imaginable assault, returning its heroes to the plenitude of earth with Mother's cups of tea and caramel slice.

*

The next photo she nudged in front of me with her finger was a postcard Kodak 100 Gold, that showed a pensive David near a lake. The sunlight is skidding on the water's ruffled foil and softens definition. His torso is baked and lean, and his chest wears a badge of incipient hair. There is a girl beside him wearing a red bikini. She is pouting a theatrical kiss, but he doesn't seem to be aware of it.

We grew together through the primary school years, attended the same secondary school, and joined the same youth group that was affiliated with the local church and therefore held an implicit didactic morality. For boys in their early and mid-teens, sex was an escalating interest, and while the church conceded sex a rightful place, beyond the sanctioned limits it was thought to be a 'sin', a word that trembled with its fire and brimstone penalties, with biblical injunctions lathered from the pulpit. It was something you could not even approach by stealth or edge enjoyably towards, for the devil triumphed over paltry human will.

David was smitten by Hilary White, a tall, reserved girl with hazel eyes, and long, wavy, light brown hair. They'd sometimes talk, but these brief meetings never attained the intimacy David needed to ask her out. We often laughed about this in our maturer years, but it was another age and another culture, an age of more stylised conventions and more fragile egos.

There's no accounting for the images that cling. Why for instance do I still recall the image of myself as a ten-year old, infatuated with the primary school girl singing 'The Holly and the Ivy' in piping soprano at the Odeon theatre, her head raised to the gods, and rarefied, the whiteness of her throat exposed. Other images leave a more indelible mark from their significance in a life, like the time David took the blame for me, and I for him, only to find it was someone else who was the culprit. Sometimes the images emerge from their drama or humour.

The most vivid recollection is the time a small group of us visited Lake Parramatta, a picturesque park where the sulphur-crested cockatoos play tag between the towering gums. David, giving a mock homily on the need for moderation, a satire on our youth group days, overbalanced and fell into the lake, sending a gliding phalanx of ducks scattering in all directions. A confusion of concern and hilarity became exclusively the latter when we found he was all right. Equal to the occasion, he rose to the surface, some green fern draped across his head, and with a sorry look, emitted a plaintive 'quack'. Of course the incident became folklore, and it became customary to greet David thereafter with a 'quack quack', and to present him with a child's rubber ducky for significant birthdays. On one such occasion, I began his birthday eulogy with a plea for moderation that captured his fateful words, much to everyone's amusement.

On a few occasions, David seemed to wear his heart on his sleeve. There were more times, though, when he feared the risky business of feeling's trade. He declared his love for me in our mid-teen years. Although frank and passionless, I asked too many questions, disconcerting him and urging grander meaning on a simple truth. Love for me then was something definite and circumscribed, revealingly daring; not something more general and expansive, more freely offered.

My burning feelings about love and friendship were part of the stew of imaginings experienced in the comfort of my first room at home with its bed and desk and reassuring books, a room from which I looked out on the world at the bright and luminous night sky, a world that made its constant claims on a teenage boy. Even the pittosporum's nutty fingers thrumming on the pane was portentous.

Bethany was the girl in the red bikini. I remember, because I had taken the photo. David met her in his first year at university. She had a glamour and *savoir faire* that was alluring, particularly for one who, like myself, had led such a cloistered life. A group of six of us was picnicking at the Basin, a ferry trip from Palm Beach. It was a happy time, swimming on a small, secluded beach, lying crumbed in the sand, eating Camembert and pâté, clambering over rocks, skinny-dipping. Not having seen that photo for many years, I held it up to the light, surprised by the pensive look on his face. Whatever could he have been thinking?

*

'This is the same one I have framed on my dressing table,' she tells me. It's a wedding print of blown-up Kodachrome, taken at St Judes, a small but historic stone church set in idyllic tree-studded grounds to the north-west of Sydney. The photo has a detail crisp enough from the Leica super zoom lens to catch the glisten of springtime showers on damask rose. Bethany shines in sun-augmented white, while David, the groom in black with scarlet cummerbund, is stilted in a cardboard pose. The photogenic grin belies the distant message in his eyes.

I don't remember anything remarkable about their courtship. There were no fiery separations and passionate reunions. They were designated 'a couple' from the early years, though I wouldn't have chosen Bethany for his partner. I have long since ceased to wonder why one's friends marry the people they do. To fathom such a complexity defies analysis, and is even beyond the powers of the two involved. I remember thinking at the time that whatever the nature of the love they felt, their years together were at least a recruitment of one another to a shared version of reality.

The weather was glorious, and the occasion was conducted in consummate style, bridesmaids in flowing burgundy, groomsmen in grey tuxedos with white carnations. The reception was held in a grand old mansion nearby with a huge dining room, a ballroom and vaulted ceilings. No expense was spared. As best man, I toasted the bride and groom, avoiding both the pablum of wedding speeches, and references to quacking ducks. David's reply quoted Donne's valediction, likening Bethany and himself to the twin legs of a compass, the 'fixed' one defining the movement of the other and leaning more towards the other the further it moves away.

Before they departed in their streamer-decked car with its 'just married' signs and trail of empty tin cans, Bethany held me close, thanking me. 'Isn't it wonderful,' she whispered, her face alight. I could feel her glow beneath the slippery satin of her gown, and the rapid beating of her heart.

David shook my hand. 'Thank you for everything,' he said. 'I mean, for all the years,' and then more cryptically, 'It went well, didn't it? Everything's as it should be.'

*

The fourth photo I'd never seen. It was a candid Instamatic shot of three fellows carousing at a barbecue with steins raised high in mock salute, a shot that lopped a waving hand, and reddened eyes like feral cats. An archetype Aussie male stands in the foreground and seems to be conducting a singing fest with tongs between turning meat. David, one of the three, is in the background, but he is not singing. His brooding eyes are dark like craters in a Grecian mask.

I look at the back of the photo, but there is no date, and nothing to identify the other two men. I assume it was taken in his early married years. Women appear to be in the background hugging wine glasses as a remedy, or dangling them in impatient fingers. Bethany isn't one of them.

David was so open with me, so full of the joy of life, but he always seemed to be searching for something more. It was only when I saw this photo that I recalled his cryptic and matter-of-fact assessment of his wedding day. Was love for him circumscribed? Did he always have to keep something in reserve, a cache for days that would never come, a natural inclination to love, yet a circumstantial will against it?

A few months after the wedding, I met an anxious Bethany for coffee, asking my opinion about the nature of love, asking about how men expressed love, asking about David. She was concerned that he didn't love her, and wanted to know if he'd ever said anything to me, if I could provide any clue to help her understand. I couldn't, and reassured her with the usual take on gender differences. I could see that she feared the peril of her own acknowledgement, that once she became convinced of her suspicion, the deluge would begin.

*

I'm surprised she kept these last two photos. Surely they could only promote unwanted memories. The Fuji colour print had been torn into jagged halves and sticky taped together. The crumple in the gutter is unmistakeably David. The flash thyristor control has lit a face that slants with shuttered eyes to the brook of ochre vomit congealed by the winter chill, and a shirt tail flags the open trouser fly where an empty amber bottle has rolled.

I fetched David from the gutter. A well-meaning passer-by found my business card in his wallet and phoned me. I don't know who took the photo, or how it ended up with his mother. But I do know that I was the one who tore it in halves.

After the failure of David's marriage, we drifted apart. But for his first year with Bethany we'd meet monthly at the same local restaurant where we'd swap stories of our first juvenile loves, and of how we must have presented like romance's bumbling heroes from an 1890s music hall, aflutter near our heroines, beneath a large membranous moon, with such unease it had to breed calamity. Yet from the worldliness that comes with age, we ridiculed the inhibition of those years, sharing our memories sipping coffee, flirting with the waitresses and discussing our feelings without shame.

David's second wife was quite the opposite of Bethany, highly intelligent, plain, disdainful of the world of glamour, and so protective, or insecure, that he was shielded from both his friends and his family. It was from the bitter decline of this relationship after many years, with its abuse and litigation over property and two young children, I heard about the voluntary insanity of his drinking.

Sometimes I saw his decline as a vagary of life. At other times I felt guilty. Could I have done more? Friends are supposed to bear each other's infirmities. David had once unlocked the feelings that I never thought legitimate between men. The feelings that were once only sparingly released in words to women with the lure of romance, and that all too often resulted in injured feelings and escalating games, were complemented by the deep and sexless bond of male companionship that toughens when there's threat. The feelings I once confessed to David were to another self.

*

I don't know how she came to be in possession of the final photo, or who might have taken it. Perhaps it was a copy of an official police record. The towers of Circular Quay float upside down in this Konica print, and a lunchtime crowd fly spots the pier for a glimpse of the body that bloats a snarl of drowning garden rubbish and the plastic detritus of sex. From a heeling launch, two policemen are using grappling hooks with the passionless mien that reminds the onlooker that this is just another day's work.

I didn't hear of his death for a few months, and still remember the shock. Death, even if it is expected, is bewildering in its impact because it's hard to accept the sudden foray into nothingness. Looking at the photo now, the pain of that first revelation returned. I could feel the blood drain from my face, and found myself studying the photo as if I needed proof, some evidence that it was David in that snarl of rubbish, or that I might see some tiny overlooked detail to shed new light.

The hardest thing to accept was David's reason behind it. There were no suspicious circumstances. To welcome death, you have to be glutted in heart, mind and spirit. Sated. Why couldn't he have turned to me? I felt bothered that he hadn't. Might he have thought that what we shared was disintegrating with the rest of his life? The death of anyone is always the concern of those who are left behind.

*

We finish our tea in silence, and she's the one who rescues me. I realise she's been watching me closely. 'It was all such a long time ago, and before you ask, yes, I'm all right. I play cards with the girls twice a week, and I go to Probus. I get a bit lonely some nights but I have the

TV and Snuggles.' The cat is purring loudly on the seat it has claimed as its own.

I leave with promises of returning soon, having to wait for the slice of carrot cake she carefully wraps in foil with arthritic fingers. The rusty gate squeals as I close it behind me.

My memory is the only shield I have against the killjoy of the fleeting years. Its preservation is a private trust, the record of both my history and identity. Sometimes I wonder if my many memories of us are just the same as his were, or whether some are fiction, made more real when thinking makes them so. Do memories always disappear with age, or do they multiply, embellished by the insights of our creeping years, to fit the meanings that we now revere, to sustain the hope that looks forward rather than backwards?

It's his turn to order and pay. It's always the same, large flat white for him, a mug of mocha for me, and a raisin toast we share.

'Make the mocha really hot,' he tells the waitress. He knows me so well.

An attractive middle-aged woman in a tailored suit strides purposefully past the restaurant.

'You haven't lost it yet. She couldn't keep her eyes off you,' David begins with his mischievous smile.

'Yes, I know. It's always the same.' I pretend to be blasé. 'But I'm quite sure she was looking at you.'

We laugh. There's no self-delusion here. It's part of our mythology.

Loyalty

She saw them from the kitchen window as she was replenishing the cheeses and pâté for her guests. They probably thought they couldn't be seen in the dark at the foot of the garden, concealed by the massive fronds of the umbrella plant, but they hadn't bargained on the prying moon that emerged suddenly from behind a cloud and bathed them in light. They were pressed close together, he with his arms around her bare shoulders, and she with her head resting against his chest. They kissed at the very moment the moon appeared.

Pru struggled through the remainder of the evening, playing the role of the consummate hostess, serving drinks and petits fours, and making polite conversation, a role that afforded her considerable pride. But she was suffering, and on the lookout for any further evidence of intimacy to confirm what she'd seen, a look or touch, or even studied avoidance. So her guests could not depart soon enough.

'Well, do you want to tell me what's going on?' she confronted him accusingly, aware that he would have had ample time to think of an excuse, because she knew he had looked up after that incriminating moment to see her face at the kitchen window.

'It really wasn't anything,' he tried to reassure, aware that he had been caught in flagrante delicto, and realising too late how lame his defence must sound. But before he had time to explain, she reacted explosively.

'Not anything. Not anything,' she repeated testily. 'You see your husband kissing your best friend, hidden, or so he believes, by the dark and among the shrubs, and he tells you it's nothing. What would *something* look like?'

'Naomi has been having marital problems,' he began warily. 'She wanted my opinion, wanted to confide without Phillip being suspicious. We walked in the garden, she took my arm, and as she was unburdening herself, she started to shake almost uncontrollably, and to cry, so we held each other. It was mutual. She needed to be comforted. After a little while, she calmed down. I was taken by surprise when she kissed me. You were looking through the window, so you would have seen that she was the one who took the initiative.'

Paul and Pru Blake had been married happily for twenty years. When many of her girlfriends referred to the stock word 'happily' to describe their marriages, they used it like a quilt that overlay the creases and blemishes in the fabric of their relationships. When Pru used the word, it referred to a relationship of give and take, of peace and contentment. Paul was her first and only love from her schooldays, and he had always been caring and considerate, indulgent of her occasional mood swings, and tolerant of her little jealousies.

'You didn't exactly pull away, though, did you? It was how many seconds…?' She still felt the pain of betrayal, but grudgingly accepted his explanation. What else could she do?

In the year that followed, Pru was tormented by what she had seen. She followed Paul to his Wednesday night ten-pin bowling with his mates, and secretly watched him. She saw him laughing and gesticulating with the seventeen-year-old schoolgirl behind the counter, but apart from that, he was with his male friends the whole time, and she didn't see anything untoward. She would hurry home guiltily to be there when he returned to ask him questions, feigning interest in what she had already witnessed.

Twice she checked on his movements by using some pretext to ring the places he said he would be, to see if he was there. When given the opportunity, she would turn out his pockets searching for damning evidence, questionable receipts, unaccounted for movie tickets, jewellery forgotten or meant as gifts, or billets-doux. She didn't find any. One day she discovered a red smear on his shirt collar, and felt ashamed by her premature attack when he sheepishly held up a half-eaten raspberry chew bar from his pocket.

In the years that followed, the residue of unease remained, and when they entertained or were entertained, she tried to isolate Naomi from Paul, but they seemed to behave as one might expect good friends, and not lovers to behave. She remembered from her university days, a Spanish poet who wrote, 'he kissed me and now I am someone else'. Perhaps Naomi had moved on, was now someone else, and Paul had been the agent of such a change. But was it possible that Paul was someone else? Beyond that kiss, she could find no real reason for suspecting that he was smitten with Naomi. She could accept that some things people say they remember might never have happened, that thinking makes them real, but she never doubted what she had seen at the foot of her garden in the moonlight. That image was indelible.

*

'He's a lovely man, Mum.' Sarah was enthusiastic and teasingly provocative. 'At least that's my impression from the only time I met him, and he's certainly rapt in you.'

'I don't think so, not in an old bag like me,' Pru countered, though she enjoyed being told of her appeal, something that she had increasingly doubted with the years. 'I'm over the hill. But Ken is a very nice man. He's been so lonely since his poor wife died, so I really hope he finds someone nice.'

'I think it's you he wants, Mum.' Sarah continued to tease her mother, never entertaining the possibility of a serious relationship. 'And what's all this about being over the hill? You're still an attractive woman. Just imagine. You have two men at your beck and call. Probably more, for all I know. You might have Dad getting jealous.'

'I've told your father about Ken and how attentive he's been,' Pru explained. 'Not that there's much to tell. It's not that anything's happened, or ever will. I thought it was important to be honest, and I really believed that he might have been concerned, even accusing, but he seemed to be pleased that another man might find me attractive.'

'That's great,' Sarah began exuberantly, but hesitated when she saw her mother's creased brow and pensive look. 'What's the matter? You don't want him to be jealous, do you?'

'It's probably silly,' Pru answered, 'but yes, I think I do. I don't want him to be miserable,' and not, she almost said, to suffer the torment that I have over all these years, 'but if he were just a little jealous, it might convince me that he really cares, that he really loves me. Doesn't being possessive and jealous amount to the same thing? I sometimes wonder if he'd like me to have some sort of liaison with another man, not necessarily an affair, but...' she was momentarily stumped for words, 'so that it would free him to do the same, like giving him a permission note to pursue other women.'

Pru had never spoken this way with her daughter before, had never revealed anything of her marriage, and Sarah was aware that the light-heartedness of their earlier conversation had become more serious, and that she was being called upon to dismiss her mother's concerns, burdens that she had not been privy to before. Perhaps there were things she didn't know.

'I have no doubt, Mum,' she began emphatically, 'that Dad is devoted to you. He may seem a little flirtatious at times,' she said with greater levity, feeling that this more oppressive mood, settling like an eiderdown over their conversation, needed to be lightened, 'but it's innocent, it's high-spirited, it's fun, it's all out in the open.'

'You're right,' Pru responded, more buoyant now. 'Just who's the parent anyway in this relationship?' and they both laughed.

'I'd be delighted,' Sarah added, if only Michael, or anyone for that matter, was as rapt in me as Dad is in you, and of course Ken too,' and she nudged Pru, who responded with a mock cautionary wagging of her finger.

Sarah and Michael had been married for several years, and while they had no children as yet, there were no apparent tensions in their relationship. Michael was reserved, though solid and dependable, and content with a conventional home life. He worked as an auditor in the city, and never seemed to get anxious or irate. Sarah seemed to be a supportive wife, affectionate and indulgent, and an efficient hostess like her mother.

'Thanks, Mum,' Sarah said quietly, visibly affected. 'I appreciate it.'

Pru nodded, and gripped her daughter's arm, conscious of their bond though not realising till some time later why she was being thanked.

*

Paul died suddenly. April the ninth. A cardio infarction. There had been no warning signs. Fifty-four years old. Pru walked beside the funeral casket, buffed to a claret gloss, a dignified veneer that separated the harsh reality of death from a life that she saw as almost unbearably capricious.

Family and friends filed out of the funeral chapel rheumy-eyed, all nursing their personal images that the opiate of sorrow couldn't dull, some casting a lingering goodbye look. Sarah and Michael clung mutely to each other. Two of Pru's ancient aunts gave affirming nods to the funeral's taste, their hair as blanched as summer cloud, and sparse as maidenhair.

Pru was quiet for months, not so much with an outpouring of grief, but more from the narcotic of suffering, an emptiness of feeling. She didn't indulge the usual incantation of bereavement, but she did dwell silently on the details of Paul's collapse, her attempts to revive him, the part played by the ambulance men, the excruciating wait at the hospital, and the telling appearance of the stony-faced doctor with the ultimate news.

On the ninth of each month, she went to the crematorium gardens and sat opposite the small bronze-plaqued niche in a brick wall that contained Paul's ashes and a parsimonious inscription. The wall was next to some contoured shrubs and pared-down roses waiting for their time, for their bloom and scent, rare seasonal solace for the departed.

And in the silence, except for the occasional slap of sprinklers fanning their manna to the dead, she'd talk to him. 'Sarah's doing another one of those university further education courses. Mrs Dodd's dog was hit by a car. The latest poll shows Labor ahead of the Liberals. Naomi and Phillip have gone to live in Byron Bay.'

In a rare moment of making her feelings more obvious, she recalled for him the proverb 'absence makes the heart grow fonder'. 'You know', she told him, 'I wonder if it must grow even more fonder when the absence is permanent.'

While she had plenty of support in her time of greatest need, no one was more attentive than Ken. He'd visit her each week, aware of not out-staying his welcome, and often bringing afternoon tea. Flowers, he thought, would be inappropriate at this early stage. He offered to go with her to the crematorium, but she politely declined, thanking him, and saying that she still needed the time alone.

After almost a year, and at an opportune moment, he indicated his feelings, not with the usual declaration, but with a statement that required no answer, that avoided confrontation. 'I think you know how I feel about you, Pru. I'm willing to wait for as long as it takes.'

She thanked him and, fully sensitive to his feelings, told him what a special person he was and how he'd been a tower of strength for her. But she didn't tell him that there would be no room in her heart for him.

When Sarah offered to accompany her to the crematorium gardens on the first anniversary of Paul's death, she gratefully accepted. Paul would like that. They sat in silence on the wooden bench that fronted the wall for several minutes. Pru felt that Sarah's presence made her usual talk to Paul unnecessary.

Sarah was briefly arrested by her father's shiny plaque, conspicuous in the wall of otherwise dulling brass plaques with hints of lichen. 'Will you keep coming every month now, Mum?' and before Pru had time to reply, 'Or do you think it might be time to move on?'

Pru knew what Sarah was hinting at, and as it made her feel

uncomfortable, she evaded the intent of the question. 'I have moved on. I'm not moping around the house any more. I'm not depressed, and I'm doing most of the things I did before. I'm sure you'd tell me if you thought I was living in some kind of illusory world.'

But Sarah persisted. 'You know what I mean, Mum. There are lots of other people out there.' She skirted the more explicit reference to men. 'You're still attractive,' and she smiled. 'I seem to remember we had this talk once before.'

'Thank you for caring, Sarah,' Pru replied, and took her daughter's hand, 'but I do know what I want, and I have everything that I need.'

Before leaving, they resumed their silence, sitting close together on the bench. The sun was casting long geometric shadows on the lawn, and the sky was the colour of lavender. Death may have isolated us, she thought, nodding towards Paul, but it's given me the certainty of life and love. It's made me see both of our lives more clearly, given them both more definition than I'd ever appreciated before.

*

When Michael returned home from the office that evening, Sarah wasn't in her usual place scurrying around the kitchen preparing the dinner and answering the quiz questions from the television in the living room.

'Sarah,' he called, but there was no answer. He climbed the stairs to find her in the bedroom packing her suitcase.

'I'm going to stay with friends for a few days,' she said peremptorily, and left with no further explanation.

Dementia

On the day after his admission, I press a knob that relaxes the tight security of the Henry Kendall Nursing Home, and a nurse opens the door. I'm taken to room 11, my father's room. From that day on, my mother would begin her daily climb the few hundred metres along a rough and furrowed clay track, lined with lantana, to the nursing home and its cushioned world among the scented gums, where my father endured the regulation meals, assisted showers and toileting.

Even now, I try to imagine the feelings that tortured her when she first brought him here, their loving fifty years of partnership reduced for him to wards of four, a single iron-framed bed and a vertical grey cabinet. 'Just bring a change of clothes,' they said, 'pyjamas, toiletries. The rest can wait.' I imagine her pulling out the old overnight bag from the closet, the one that had seen some exotic escapades, neatly folding the underwear and spare shirt, perhaps holding them to her tearful face to smell his odour, the essence of their lifetime of intimacy. And lying guiltily alone in the empty bed that first night, unable to sleep, not trespassing on the side that is and would always be his, wondering what demons were visiting his new snore-filled room.

My father's tilted in the bed and staring fixedly ahead. The crumbs around his mouth are evidence of tea and biscuits, standard fare before a meagre lunch of sandwiches and fruit. By the bed opposite, a man rocks on a chair, bent so far forward that his head almost touches the floor. Another snores, turned towards the wall. The third, a surly-looking obese man who's only there for temporary respite, is playing with his radio. He doesn't seem to belong.

'Reg,' a nurse calls good-humouredly, taking the arm of a naked man who passes the door, perplexed, his penis like a long dead

Esmeralda rose nested in some desiccated leaves. The nurse smiles at me as they pass, a 'you know what it's like' smile.

This assortment of dislocated lives, inertia, vacant looks and plaintive calls, the wandering naked relics, is now my father's surreal world that scorns the code of sanity. It's here he must eke out his twilight months or years, this man who was once proud monarch in his sacred realm.

'How are you, Dad?' I open with false cheer, drawing a plastic chair noisily across the linoleum. 'Are you comfortable?'

What else can I say? No point talking about the goings-on here. He wouldn't know. Sport and politics are forever lost. So I chatter about the details of my life, my work challenges, the children's activities, the chore of painting the house, increasingly feeling like the dinner-party bore. Still, it's more comfortable than unnerving silence. I'm not sure if he's listening, but he does seem to watch me with his soft blue eyes.

'I think I'll like it here,' he whispers, barely audible.

My raw heart lurches with a tenderness, and the regrets resurface for all the things I could have done, for all those small antipathies that crawl beneath the fabric of a pleasant family life, like the sullen protest of this youthful idealist, at all his father might have done to repay his mother's selflessness, until I saw him as a victim too of time and culture's pitiless conspiracy. It's these smaller things and not the rooted sorrows that are the hardest to confess.

*

Memory is not often volitional, and often latches onto the unremarkable, perhaps images or symbols of deeper realities that were, or might have been. I think of those weekend mornings with him in the half-acre garden, digging new plots or forever weeding, thrashing the clods of rich black soil against the spade to free the weeds and bloated worms. I've always found something honest in the earth, something tough and elemental. And there's integrity in toil. It was a time of communion, with each other and the natural world. Between long silences, sweetened by the musical gratitude of magpies that gathered around us in their search for disturbed insects, he would share his insights, his spade an orator's prop, and a garden bed his stage. His muscular legs gleamed with the sheen of sweat. And we'd clasp the mugs of morning tea my mother brought us on a tray, holding them in earthy hands like chalices so they wouldn't spill.

His appeal to reason mirrored the need for fair-mindedness and justice, a stance he enacted throughout his life, and in the punishments he meted out to his sons. I only realised later how much he valued my coming to him with an issue or problem. Reason could overcome, and all could be resolved or forgiven. He'd never make the approach himself, even if my distress were obvious. He was the master of the house, and in my maturing years I became a little resentful of this vestige of Victorianism.

Images of him still curl and cling for a moment like holograms: pontifical as he makes a speech, laughing as he relates a humorous family mishap, grimacing as he endures a dispute with his sister, intent as he readies himself to bowl, serious as he scans the share prices in the morning paper, delighted as the family dog that he has lovingly groomed is given best in breed.

Where's it gone, the power, the insight, the reason and reasonableness? Or has it really gone? Perhaps it's biding its time, dormant or defying expression. He seems so helpless now, and it's not the feigned helplessness that his two sons enjoyed wrestling, clambering over him squealing, over 'the pineapple truck' as they called him for some reason that is long lost from the family culture.

*

I've heard that a large percentage of stroke victims acquire dementia within a few years. We'll never know if my father was part of that percentage. My parents had come to Henry Kendall Village a few years before, a retirement complex that boasted levels of care: conventional unit living, hostel accommodation in which meals were cooked and served, and a nursing home. There was also a pool, a bowling green, a tennis court, a library, and devotions conducted each week by a local minister.

Their top-floor unit in a block of four overlooked a putting green and the tennis court. For a while, an archery club assembled below. My mother frequented the hairdressing salon each week, a rare hour of indulgence, the fruits of retirement, and they both played bowls, my father using a metal contraption down which he could roll his bowls. Once a week, my mother would drive rather than catch the village bus to the Wyoming shops, though how she managed to return intact, I shudder to think.

I visited with my partner at least every fortnight, and stayed for the weekend, using their place as a base to visit the nearby beaches. They relished the Saturday night takeaway we bought from the Wyoming Chinese, like children having a birthday party at McDonalds.

Despite rehabilitation, my father never fully recovered from the stroke. A little freedom had developed in the muscled legs that were less tractable, reducing him to a slow-shoe shuffle, like a broken toy without a spring. We placed children's yellow plastic floaties on his arms to keep him buoyant in the pool. His walking stick confirmed the riddle of the sphinx.

It's hard to say when the dementia began. Its onset is insidious, beginning with confusion and memory loss. We all think we've succumbed when we wander into a room and wonder why, or when we can't remember a name. In the early stages, he persevered in arguing cherished notions, with non sequiturs on politics and fractured arguments on a variety of social issues, the mad conductor *sans* baton with his arms raised high like a tortured entreaty. In a few months, he was unable to turn on the television or to determine which way to wheel the walker.

In a lifetime of confederacy, my father and mother used to tease each other and laugh, disputing who was boss, but it wasn't long before the mantle became my mother's, and he complied without dissent, as long as he could work out how. She'd chatter to him as she cut his breakfast toast in easy bites, and as she gave him his morning shave, dabbing some lotion on his nose to sustain the ritual of a joke. Lukewarm morning tea was served in half-full double-handled mugs to avoid scalding and spilling, and she would wipe the leavings from his mouth. Increasingly, my mother would have to fetch the bleach to clean the shower from a not-so-savoury accident. But she never complained.

Their late-afternoon walk was therapy beside the dusk's long-fingered shade. I can still see him steering his walker with a dogged grimace stencilled on his face, and her gentle guiding hand resting on his arm.

In a rare vulnerable moment, she confided that what she missed most was not so much the freedom of not having to watch over his safety every minute of the day, but his unresponsive warmth as she held him in their bed, and her distant memories of the looks, the words, the forgotten touch that even now would settle for an instant in her mind to zigzag off like butterflies.

'Isn't it time, Mum?' I recall asking on several occasions, sensing the growing exhaustion she tried to disguise.

Relatives and well-meaning neighbours intervened, revealing options she might take, to which she'd retort, 'It may not be obvious, but this is what real love is all about.'

Yet there are certain practicalities of living that are even too daunting for love to overcome.

*

On my second visit several days later, I'm greeted by the manager at the door, sunny and convivial, a dapper little man who asks me who I'm here to visit, and who ushers me along the corridor making polite conversation about the innovations planned for the home, pointing to a large room, and leaving me at the door with 'Let me know if we can help,' before he strides away with an air of importance.

Beyond the muddled sticks and walking frames that half-block the entrance, a motley fraternity is propped, their faces empty as fallow fields or settled in accord. The television mutes false cheer, but no one is looking. Their images are private ones with more repeats than *I Dream of Jeannie*. Do they think wives back into this bankrupt room? It's hard to tell, for the faces are unreadable in each lucent, mauve-veined head.

If watched clocks never move, then time is squandered here, unhindered in its sprinting flight by ticking hands that measure lives against eternity. What lurks behind the vacant looks? Do words forget to form themselves, a mouldering partnership with thought to leave the speaker inarticulate; or have they experienced it all before, so enter time beyond all words where thoughts are finite after all, and nothing's left for them to know or feel, so nothing need be said?

My father's here, part of the human silence, staring ahead, hair neatly combed and soft blue eyes blank. He's even less reactive to my visit than a few days ago, retreating without the bugle's call.

'How are you, Dad?' And even though I try to whisper, my voice sounds stentorian.

My father doesn't answer, yet numerous others do, a miscellany of 'wells' and 'thank yous'. In retrospect I'll laugh, seeing this as black comedy or farce, but at the time it was poignant.

Once, he'd loved to talk and I'd find the tendentiousness irritating. He'd listen to an argument and deliberately oppose it, quite apart from what he really thought. But what I once found annoying, his silence and the lifelessness of the room, except for the just audible canned hysterics from the television, had made somehow endearing. It was something quintessentially 'him'. The treasured books I'd lovingly covered in plastic as an early teen, and that he allowed me to keep on my modest bedroom bookcase, included the works of Darwin, Kant and Descartes, perhaps the basis of his love for disputation.

I remember finding his service medals, long interred inside a drawer of bric-a-brac, tape measures, pens, sharpeners and bulldog clips, that revived memories of the almost forgotten memoirs of his war time travels in the Middle East, the smudged and furry copies typed lovingly on my mother's Remington, accounts I'm ashamed to say I'd never read.

I'm rescued by a nurse who enters with the morning tea on a trolley, dodging the walking frames.

'Time flies,' I offer emptily, ashamed at once of seeming trite.

'But surely time stands still,' she says surprised, 'and we're the ones who fly.'

I watch as arthritic fingers claw at mugs and, with their backs turned on the future, watch time's present rush away to inundate a cluttered past.

I let my hand rest on my father's shoulder, feeling its barely padded boniness. 'Keep well,' I whisper. 'I'll come again soon,' and I use the nurse's return as my opportunity to leave. 'Please thank the manager,' I ask her, and after a moment of seeming baffled, she laughs at my surprise.

'The manager isn't here today. I can see you've met our Ted.' She smiles. 'He's just another patient here. He used to be the mayor of Ryde.'

Donegal

Donegal first spoke to Tom one bleak November afternoon. And from that moment, Tom was well aware what people would think. This fellow thinks a dog can talk. But he was prepared to suffer it all – the nods in his direction, the whispering behind cupped hands, the fingers initially raised to point, then respectfully diverted to rub a nose or scratch an ear. And it wasn't the fertile imagination of the doting mother who swears her infant said 'Dada' when it merely gurgled.

Donegal's first words were erudite and deeply resonant. 'The literature review was superb, but her treatment of the methodology was slight. I'm not sure she understands Miles and Huberman.'

Tom had been marking an Honours thesis, and Donegal's comments rang true.

'Yes, I can talk,' he answered Tom's incredulous stare. There was mischief in those doe-soft amber eyes, and he began to laugh good-naturedly, his meaty tongue lolling back and forth like wipers on a car.

The twilight sun splashed into the room and lit his copper fur.

'But you never spoke before.' Tom hovered in that zone of disbelief, waiting for fantasy to declare itself. But there was no one else at home. It was no hoax.

Donegal uncurled himself from the floor, and strode upright to the armchair, where he sat down cross-legged. 'I haven't felt the need till now,' he said reflectively. 'Besides, it becomes galling for an intelligent Irish setter to remain silent to "Donny-wonny want a bikkie?" or "Donny want to go walkies?"'

'I'm really sorry Don… Donegal.' Tom sensed the absurdity of his apology and went no further. Then he felt sad and guilty. This was an intelligent creature who understood the qualitative analysis of Miles and Huberman, and who'd been relegated to leashes, nightly walks, raw bones and a kennel.

'Don't worry about it, Tom,' he smiled. It's hard to gauge expressions from such a proboscis, but there was no 'master', or 'Mr Ellis', but 'Tom'. Names position relationships. They define role and status, and this was a signal of equality. 'Can I get you a coffee?' And before Tom could answer, he strode to the kitchen, filled the kettle, and began to apportion coffee and milk in two mugs.

That night, Tom emptied the junk from the spare room. 'I want Donegal to have his own room,' he told his disbelieving wife. 'A soft bed to sleep in, a table to work at, and his own books.'

His wife was very caring for the next few days, diverting the children, bringing him breakfast in bed, insisting that he sit and read or watch television while she stroked his forehead, and even walking Donegal. Tom felt sure that Donegal gave him a complicit wink that first night as he trotted off compliantly.

As an academic, Tom was trained to not accept things at face value. He wasn't alone with Donegal in the house for a few days, so he used the opportunity wisely. He researched the ways words are produced from the speech organs, the modification of air moving under pressure from the lungs by the vocal cords, soft palate, teeth, teeth ridge, hard palate, tongue and lips. He discovered how the palatal fricative 'X' is sounded when the front of the tongue is raised near enough to the hard palate to create audible friction, and how the velar fricative occurs when the back of the tongue is raised near enough to the soft palate. It just wasn't possible! And he studied comparisons of human and canine brains, the function and relative sizes of cerebellum, cerebrum, hypothalamus, corpus callosum and corpus striatum. No, it wasn't possible! But the next few weeks, and years, would challenge such scientific certainty.

*

The coming out of Donegal was a cautious and deliberate process. First there was the family to convince. 'Now I don't want you to think I'm mad,' Tom began, and realised he'd planted a prolific harvest. What else could they think? But Donegal came to the rescue, demonstrating the range of his talents. The children were delighted. They had another brother, ready-made, playful and not demanding parental attention. Donegal was sensitive, indulgent and patient. His guile in bowling leg spin and the flipper would sometimes irritate Tom's son if he was dismissed with successive deliveries, but Donegal proved a master of diplomacy.

His wife was a different proposition. As a mere dog, Donegal was lovable. As an intelligent male of indeterminate age, he was suspect. It may have been his manhood, more manifest now that he insisted on walking upright, that unnerved her. Perhaps it was the shift in power. You can cuddle a child. Its desires and needs are malleable. But you can't as readily fondle a grown male, particularly when there is no consanguinity as defence.

While she supported Tom in his plans for Donegal, her relationship with him became more restrained. Her affection wasn't as demonstrable and she spoke to him with the urbanity you afford a visitor rather than a family member. She never walked him again, and yet for that Tom was secretly grateful.

One of his fondest memories was running with Donegal. They'd go at night so Donegal could run upright, and they'd discuss the latest novels of Saramago, Marquez and Philip Roth. But there was never a time that his wife wanted Donegal at the table when they entertained friends for dinner, even though he was the perfect model of decorum, and could explain the culinary predilections of all the royal courts in Europe.

The second phase in Donegal's coming out was to reveal his secret to a wider circle. To the chagrin of Tom's wife, it polarised their friends. Some thought it marvellous. It appealed to either science or the absurd. Tom's close friend, a devotee of Bertrand Russell, was delighted, claiming it turned the world on its head.

Others were disturbed that it challenged a cherished natural order, and one woman was disgusted. 'A dog is a dog is a dog,' was all her intellect allowed. 'If you think I'm going to sip cucumber soup at the table with a, with a…' and they never saw her again.

Donegal was equal to the adulation and denunciation. He seemed above it all except for one black day. The husband of a lifelong friend of Tom's wife was crudely decrying the lack of female talent in his workplace. 'And as for Yvonne,' he mocked, 'she's a real dog.'

Donegal's copper fur bristled. His eyes lost their sheen. Tom could see his tension as he sat next to him sipping his Chardonnay.

'I think you'd better apologise,' Donegal said icily.

'Don't worry, mate,' the man laughed. 'It's a figure of speech, just an expression.'

Tom still nurses an image of the man's flight down the river pebble drive at Dural, with an upright Irish setter, eyes agleam, brandishing a baseball bat in hot pursuit, and gaining with every stride.

*

Donegal sat for the Higher School Certificate with Tom's son. He did the same subjects by correspondence, though he did have to formally sit the examination. There was some consternation among the invigilators when Donegal took his seat, arranged his pens on the desk and donned his reading glasses. One girl was carried from the room shrieking with uncontrollable mirth.

Universities accept candidates to degree courses by UAI scores. So it was that Donegal was accepted into teacher education at the university. Again there were hiccups at enrolment.

'But you're a dog,' the wide-eyed woman said at the enrolment station.

'Yes,' Donegal replied matter-of-factly.

'But…' The woman was flustered. 'It doesn't say so on the application form.'

Donegal took the form deftly in his paw. 'You're quite right,' he said officiously, 'and there's no place for anyone to indicate whether or not they're Homo sapiens. In fact,' Donegal pressed home his advantage, 'there's nothing here to indicate whether applicants are porcine, canine, feline, equine, bovine, wolverine or simian.'

Equity provisions were firmly entrenched at the university. Applicants couldn't be excluded on the basis of race, background, gender or disability. There was no formal provision to cover Donegal, though the spirit of the policy was clear, and a dog-loving vice chancellor decided to take the risk.

Incredulity, caution, novelty and acceptance were the stages in Donegal's adoption by the students. After initial bewilderment, they began to talk to him, tentatively at first and then wholeheartedly. It became desirable to work on group assignments with Donegal or to sit with him in the refectory. Even when the novelty had gone, Donegal's great compassion and brilliant scholarship made him a favourite.

Practice teaching proved the stumbling block. The day started badly and grew worse. Tom arrived at Lindfield Public School with Donegal, upright, a new leather briefcase in his paw. A dog-catcher had just locked a nondescript terrier in his wire-caged utility. Tom saw the dog's furtive glance at Donegal, the downcast look of the victim, and felt unusually sad.

'Bloody circus dog, is it?' the dog catcher called, looking pointedly at the 'No Dogs on Premises' sign, and back to Tom before he turned to his ute.

'Up yours, feller,' Donegal growled in a tone that belied his usual equanimity.

'What did you say? What did you bloody say?' The man approached, puce and bellicose, fists clenched, and standing with his face centimetres from Tom's.

'On yer bike, feller…or I'll bite yer backside.' Donegal was enjoying himself.

The man swung round to look at Donegal. Then he wheeled to look at Tom…and back to Donegal. Right, left, right to cross reality's divide. 'I'll bloody well…I'll bloody…' And, lost for words, he retreated.

The school principal was a gentle soul, but terrified of crossing the departmental line. 'I really can't put you in a classroom,' he explained, at least affording Donegal the courtesy of direct address. 'If the department says it's all right…' and an urgent meeting was convened with the department that afternoon.

Soames was a malevolent man who thrived on creating obstacles. He'd pore over precedent or legal definition, and take gratuitous delight in promoting uncertainty and pain. As life had clearly not been kind to him, his retaliation was indiscriminate.

A magnificently groomed and handsome dog with a Boss briefcase, and demonstrable culture and erudition, was a new challenge. Difference was to be feared; superiority detested. 'There's a regulation,' he was snide, 'about animals in schools. You're clearly an *animal*,' and he savoured the word.

Tom and Donegal parried by reading the equity provision in the *Teachers' Handbook*, and the anti-discrimination legislation.

Soames was not deterred. 'There's a regulation,' he whined, 'about school staff wearing appropriate attire. If I'm not mistaken…' he was revelling in his cleverness, 'you don't have any attire at all. Not to put too fine a point on it, you're nude.' The word was pronounced 'nyood', and with all the relish of the infant boy's incipient use of 'bum'.

Donegal remained calm and with not the slightest hint of self-consciousness. 'The significant word, Mr Soames,' he retorted politely, 'is "appropriate". It would be most inappropriate for a dog to dress. If he were to do so, he'd be accused of aping humans, if you'll excuse the pun. If you wish to enforce that regulation, you'll be vilified by Animal Liberation.'

'There's a regulation,' Soames began again, unmollified. And so they traversed the minefield of department regulations governing professional image, duty of care, and relationships with staff and children. Soames even threatened to consult an actuary. If every human year, he argued, is equivalent to seven dog years, then Donegal would have to pay seven times the normal superannuation contribution, and that would leave him no salary at all.

Donegal didn't become a teacher, at least not in a school. But his months of work were not for nought. His reputation for scholarship was such that the university offered him a research position that also involved a small teaching allocation. His output of research papers was prodigious and his talents as a teacher were vaunted.

*

'You look really tired, Don,' Tom said.

They'd been watching *Madame Bovary* together after the family had retired to bed. Donegal was sitting on his reclining chair, his legs apart and his nose erect. His eyes had rolled back to reveal their whites, and the glasses had fallen from his snout. He'd been snoring, a low gravelly rumble.

'You've been pushing too hard.'

'No, it's not that,' he replied wearily. 'There's something I have to tell you.'

Donegal wasn't one for proclamation. He was normally so understated that Tom sensed the portentous. Gobs of rain dashed the window from a galvanic sky. There was the tell-tale eerie silence that precedes revelation.

'I'm not young any more.'

Tom smiled. 'Not young. You're only eight.' He was relieved and even dismissive.

'No, let me go on. I'm older than you. I'm fifty-six. I am tired. I have arthritis in my tail, and standing erect has played havoc with my lower back. I reckon on four good years…four of your years. The last year at the university's been great, but I have to make fresh plans.'

Tom felt an extraordinary sadness. There was a slight greying around his snout. His teeth had muddied a little and his amber eyes were a paler honey. Tom had faced his own mortality, but never another's, and it was hurtling towards them. Tom wanted to hug Donegal but didn't move. Was it his own very humanness, the veneer of seemliness that held his instincts in check? Was it Donegal's barely quasi-humanness that curbed his response? Or was it Donegal's greater benignity that gave Tom pause? What he felt for him now ran deeper than master and loyal servant. He was wise counsel and compassionate friend.

'I want to devote the rest of my life,' Donegal continued, 'to my own kind. I've been selfish. Now it's time to give other dogs the chances I've had.' He could see Tom's pain and lightened the mood. 'Every dog has his day,' he quipped and laughed.

'Why not let sleeping dogs lie?' Tom challenged.

And so they retired to bed.

After one of those nights when the mind permits the body no rest, Tom rose early and went to Donegal's room with a litany of questions. He wasn't there. The bed hadn't been slept in. And he wasn't downstairs cooking breakfast.

'Donegal,' he called.

There was no answer.

'Donegal.'

After the third call, Tom saw him emerging from the kennel on all fours. 'Donegal.' Tom ran to him. 'Is everything all right?'

There was no answer.

'Aren't you going to speak to me?'

Donegal wagged his tail and ambled to the nearest azalea to lift his leg.

Tom made the usual breakfast of bacon and eggs. Donegal showed no interest and would only eat the dried dog food of yesteryear. He didn't go to work and he didn't return to his room.

Later that day, Tom fetched his old leash, hopeful that he would confide on their nightly run. He didn't.

He never spoke again. He never walked upright. Instead, he disappeared during the day and often overnight, returning dishevelled and exhausted. Even as the months became years, Tom didn't relent, using their times alone to speak to him.

At first, Tom inquired, pleading for affirmation. Then he simply offered his support. 'If there's anything I can do,' or related the events of his day at university. 'You'll never believe what MacFarlane did.' Tom still doesn't know if he listened. He certainly gave no impression of doing so.

*

The day Donegal died was bleak and grey like most July days. The pallid morning was thawing with anaemic colour. Tom found him sphinx-like in the kennel, his head on his paws, and his eyes vacant. He was grateful that Donegal was at least spared capture and summary execution.

The family gathered to bury him that morning in the backyard. That's what he would have wanted. Tom remembers bundling him into his arms, and staggering with his weight, his copper fur ablaze in the winter sun, and his legs splayed like palings hanging off a fence. The family stood around his grave, and they each said a few words. There was no invocation of theology or talk of doggie paradise.

The family members went on each of their weekend ways, and Tom remained alone for what he knew would be a time of painful self-indulgence and catharsis. He had to confront the profound sense of loss he couldn't explain. He needed to feel his feelings, and allow the pain to spill his understanding. And there was guilt to resolve. Surely he could have done more.

The storm arrived mid-afternoon, heralded by black scudding cloud that switched off the sun, and lightning that knifed the dark. Tom thought it biblical, nature's underscoring of the momentous. The initial ferocity abated in several minutes, but the rain continued to fall heavily.

There was a faint scratching at the family room door, and through the glass Tom could see a forlorn-looking cocker spaniel, sodden and shivering. Inside was safe haven. He opened the door and closed it quickly against the elements. She stood in a growing puddle of water on the entrance tiles, not daring to shake herself. Tom went for a towel.

'Thank you so much,' she said with a dulcet voice. 'Beastly weather.'

And Tom knew the visit was no accident.

Twilight

Twilight, and sparkle from a low, rising moon tapers towards them across a dozing ocean. The bottom of the sky is apricot and lilac. They're standing, looking across the water, silent. Nothing they could say could capture the immensity of beauty. Nothing they are able to articulate could capture what's growing between them.

Unlocking their hands, he kneels on the hardened sand that the receding water has smoothed, and scrawls a message, the hard-wet letters bold in the displaced sand: the subject 'I', self-conscious now in her presence, and tethered to an 'l', hurrying to a generous 'o', the symbol he knows of her sex, to 'v' that plunges to a hesitant cusp before his finger's quick ascent and glide to 'e'. He stands, his knees crumbed with sand, moves a few paces away, and inscribes 'you', the other side of love beyond himself.

She smiles, takes his hand and is about to speak, words he is anxious to hear, hoping for a message to match the sentiment he's just revealed, when a sudden wind blows up, and darkness that isn't night comes sprinting across the sky. The horizon has changed colour to be pestered by a mist of slate grey, and already his inscription is pocked by gobs of rain.

'There's nowhere...' she calls out with alarm, leaving the sentence unfinished as they both start to run back along the beach.

The guest house is several hundred metres away, and there is no shelter, no cave, no shop awning. It begins to pour, a temper of autumn rain, and deep puddles are already gathering in the street, water is swirling in the gutters. Running ahead, he keeps turning to take her hand, even though he realises that such a gesture is no help at all.

At the guest house door, he can't help but laugh. A light-heartedness from adventure perhaps, something comic in what has happened, or a bizarre defence against a more dreaded concern that their first real time away together may have been spoiled. He'd often laughed before when laughter was the least appropriate response. She's standing unsmiling, her hair lank and dripping down her face. Her clothes are pasted to her body, and carry the doggy smell of sodden wool.

'I'll have to wash my hair,' is the best her annoyance allows, indifferent to her steady dripping on the floor of the tiled foyer.

'I thought you'd just done that,' he quips, now so committed to levity that it seems the only way forward, yet at the same time fearing that it might antagonise.

'The soup of the day is minestrone,' he reads nervously from the tattered menu in their room, filling the awkward silence. 'That with some hot buttered toast would go down well.'

She doesn't speak, busy removing her wet clothing. The silence persists.

'We're just so lucky,' he finally says abstractedly.

Several seconds pass before she turns to face him, and there are tears in her eyes. 'Yes, we are,' she agrees, and pulls him to her, standing with him in a drenched embrace.

He isn't sure what made her change, why some words, some messages in the most unlikely of situations, act like struck matches, lighting an emotion like they brighten a black room. But he is grateful.

'A fine spot you got me into,' she laughs. 'I think you planned the whole thing.'

'You sound like Laurel and Hardy,' he retorts, and mimics Hardy: 'A fine spot you got me into, Stan. Anyway, I did my best to rescue a damsel in distress.'

'And who was in distress?' she teases. 'You were running around out there like a chook without its head.'

'Bath time for you,' he orders, 'before we soak Mrs Willoughby's carpet,' and with her stockinged feet standing on top of his, and her arms still around his neck, he walks her laughing to the old chipped enamel bath that stands on clawed feet as if it's going to walk out the door. 'Leave the water in for me when you've finished,' and he turns on the groaning tap with instantly steaming water.

It's a long while before she emerges, wrapped in a towel, pink from the heat, perfumed with lavender, and somehow softer than before, no longer sinewy and toughened by the storm.

'My turn,' he says, and notices the puzzled way she looks at him, her head slightly tilted, and biting her lip. He thinks better of asking, evading what he senses would be a non-committal reply.

Is it the heat from the bath, he wonders, or was it a blush, the crack in carapace's long restraint, the storm a harbinger of rites of passage they would later share together in the lumpy double bed with words that tumbled hot and wet. This was no fantasy, he'd later tell himself. Some may well create the beauty of a waterfall from a lifeless stream, but this image would remain the same, inviolate.

*

Twilight, and the street lights come on, a time when the constraints of day are relieved by the liberty that bridges day from the suspense of night. A man is on the beach below, too far away from his window's view of the world to make out his features, probably middle-aged. The man treads wearily, heavily towards the water's edge and stops, looking out to sea, the burden of his world imprinted by his bare feet in the sand.

From the window, he is acutely aware of the man's misery, as if there is some mysterious floating text above his head. The waves rush at him, licking his feet with cowardly tongues before retreating. The tangerine and lilac sky, seen from another beach a year ago, are not here now. The ocean and sky are a uniform grey.

The man sits cross-legged, kneels briefly as if in prayer, and stands again, raising his arms before cradling his head in both hands, running his fingers through his hair, and gazing towards the horizon as if entreating it, a silent vocabulary of despair. A moon is high overhead, but pale as if it doesn't want to be there.

'You're always looking out,' she says, though not unkindly. 'Or perhaps I should say, beyond. I sometimes think you're out there somewhere, and not here at all. Why don't you speak to me?' she says without a trace of emotion. 'What do you hope to find?'

The man is still standing facing the ocean, his arms by his side, slumped, somehow defeated.

'Just looking at the great silent theatre of the world,' he replies, and instantly regrets being flippant. But what can he say? He could call her to the window and point out the man, ask her what she sees, what she intuits, feels, what she really knows. If she could understand, whether she is told or not, how the man hauls his torment about, he knows she'd say, with the stock cliché that's as dull as the dusk-oily sea, 'It's simply life's rich tapestry.' It's not her fault, he tells himself. Why be critical of her for not seeing what I see? This is my reality.

'I've got my yoga class in an hour,' she tells him. 'I'll eat when I get home. The casserole is heating in the oven, timed for seven. You don't have to wait.' She is searching for her purse and door keys, goes to fetch her leotard. 'Oh, and in case you're in any doubt, I'll need the four-wheel drive tomorrow. For Casey. You do remember, don't you? Now don't forget to take the rubbish out.'

She pauses at the door, gives him an uncertain look. He's still standing by the window, only paying her divided attention. 'At least by the time I get home, it'll be too black for you to see anything out there.' There's no edge to the remark. Perhaps a hint of concern. She pauses again, as if something needs to be said, but thinks better of it, turns abruptly and is gone.

He hears the car engine purr. Feels relief. And loneliness.

The man turns from the water and looks towards the road. And from the window, he flattens his hand upright against the pane, the fingers pressed together in sad salute, but the man cannot see, and is slowly moving away, picking his way through the seaweed to the street. As twilight merges into night, darkness hides the density of pain.

*

Twilight, and they seem unusually fond of each other. 'Unusually', because the last year has not seen much affection, or little emotion of any sort. They've spoken about it, though not at length, and without hostility. They were both surprised by how amicable that final talk was, how little had to be discussed. There were no recriminations.

'I'm sure you feel like me,' he told her. 'Stale, empty of passion. Whatever happened? Why has it all gone to sleep?'

She did feel like him. He must have seen her eyes, the eyes he once loved to look into, even to touch, running the pad of his fingers round the lashes and eyebrows, eyes that now betrayed an emptiness. She knew that time now would never allow them the prodigality they once knew, the drenched embrace, the steaming bath and the night of the storm. It was time to go their separate ways.

'So let's enjoy the final moments we can share.' She knew he'd comply. 'We'll have a final walk through the park.' And as if there needed to be a reason, 'There's no point moping about the past, or dwelling on what might have been. There might even be some pleasant memories we can share.' Yet as they prepare to go, her false cheer cannot hide their sadness.

The coolness of the fading day sees several families packing up their picnic things, and warning the children not to leave their skateboards or scooters behind. Sweets are offered as rewards for the well behaved. Threats are handed out for the recalcitrant. The park's playground whirligig is slowly spinning to a stop where a boy has recently jumped clear. An inverted ice cream cone oozing melted strawberry on the grass suggests a story of childhood tantrums.

They walk together yet alone beneath a canopy of trees that hides the last hurrah of lemon sun, the shut-out light seeming to subdue talk of vanishing love. Perhaps it's a blessing, he thinks, for too much sentiment is beguiling, and a herald of false hope. Emerging from the trees, the dying sun lights her auburn hair and for a moment weakens his resolve. He feels irritable, annoyed, not with her, but with the caprice of emotion that robs the precious and leaves it sterile, and with a world that allows it to happen.

She begins to dance to a music only she can hear, but it's forced and her heart isn't in it, so she stops almost before she's begun. He walks behind her, saddened rather than cheered. And at the base of a huge oak tree, she stops, scoops up an armful of freshly fallen leaves, still crisp with autumnal reds and golds, and showers them over him, her laughter overwrought.

They look at each other searchingly, and even she's surprised. She removes a leaf from his shoulder, and one that's stuck in his hair. Studies it as if it has some meaning. There's no laughter now. The moment is too portentous. And without a sign from either, they hold each other, a final sexless embrace.

'I just feel so sad that it's gone,' she says, and he can feel the wetness of tears against his cheek. 'Do you think there'll be other loves for us?'

The question is so ingenuous, he feels strangely protective.

They're silent for a long while, still clinging to each other.

'They say love conquers all,' he eventually says. 'I just wish…' and he thinks better of it, and pauses. Besides, he knows she can finish the sentence. 'I really hope it smiles on both of us.'

*

Twilight, and he walks through the park, the same route home from work he takes each weekday. In his briefcase are the documents he plans to work on that night, and the gift of an amethyst pendant for his wife. Even from a distance, there is something familiar about the woman in bottle green sitting on the park bench, and as he moves nearer, he knows there can be no mistake.

She seems a little thickened by the years, her face fluted by the sun. But it's the eyes of indigo that give her away, the eyes that ushered in each day for over a year a lifetime ago, and the auburn hair that once fringed her waist, now cropped with tongues of silver grey.

Surprised hellos and false cheer precede the clichés of 'How long's it been?' and 'Fancy seeing you.'

She stands, and after the briefest hug, a mandate of the missing years, they begin to count back the time, as furtive memories stalk like ghostly shadows. Twenty years of lives are etched in sparing detail. Her eyes that once lit desire are now becalmed, and the last rays of disappearing sun flare the faintest down above her lip.

He feels uneasy, wants to get away, but politeness bids him stay. They're strangers passing in the park, more strangers even than those who've never met, because the difference between the before and now is so bewildering. Sentiment has long since gone to sleep. Their binding words in bedroom dark are long forgotten. His leg locks with another now when he sleeps. The time to weep has long passed. She mentions children's names. Raises them like flags on sacred land. But he resists talking of shared posterity, hoping she will not say 'They might have been yours too.' She doesn't.

It all seems so unreal, from love to pain to nothingness, renewal's edict not to feel too much. We're different now, he wants to tell her, but of course she knows that. Our lives are chunked like chapters in a book, he tells himself, where complicated plots evolve and all the characters reinvent themselves.

Making excuses, he leaves, conscious of being watched until a bend in the path conceals him, saddened by the meeting as if some vague and disconcerting script is hovering above his head. She too feels uneasy, musing as he strides away, watching the young man old or old man young. She'll sit a while and thread her way through pinched feelings, pensive for a day.

Meek

'I want you to do my second-half lunch duty Mr Meek,' Florence Rouse boomed. Everything was loud and abrasive with Florence. There was no such thing as a whispered confidence. The whole staffroom was privy to every instruction, every transaction.

'But I have a recess duty, Florence,' Malcolm Meek feebly protested.

'Then you'll have first-half for lunch, won't you,' came the peremptory response. 'The principal has asked me to investigate the theft of the new Sony smart television. It cost two thousand dollars and hadn't even been taken out of the box.'

So that's her lame excuse, Malcolm thought. Several of the staff, working quietly at their desks, looked across sympathetically at Malcolm and shrugged. They were used to the same treatment.

I can't remember hating anyone, Malcolm thought, but Florence has certainly put my good nature to the test. She rides roughshod over everyone, makes all our business her own, shouts her opinions and orders whether they are personal concerns or not, and why are we all called by our surnames? Is it because she can't abide the risky business of intimacy? Is it an attempt to keep things professional, a distancing ploy?

Malcolm had been teaching history at St Edmund's, a small yet prestigious private school, for twenty years. He was well liked by Pennyworth, the principal, by the other staff and the students. A single man, he had never married, and lived a staid and predictable life. He was content to return home to walk his dog, prepare his simple meal, and to resume writing his history of the Peloponnesian Wars, a task that had already taken five years. He was friendly with the other teachers, but didn't socialise, not smoking or drinking alcohol like his colleagues.

'Meek by name and meek by nature,' one of the teachers had quipped affectionately, and it had caught on.

Perhaps his meekness was a blessing in disguise. Florence Rouse had been appointed deputy principal at the beginning of the year, brought in by Mr Pennyworth, an ineffectual principal nearing a merciful retirement, as a possible successor. Her immediate mission was to 'clean up the place' and to improve ailing standards, and to that end, she had fired three teachers. The staff was unable to see any rhyme or reason in the dismissals. They were not the poorest teachers. Schools have a rough understanding of the quality of their teachers just as teenage boys have a pecking order based on physical prowess. Todd Greenberg was an effective PE teacher, but outspoken on a variety of professional matters. Jane Dyson, an attractive young English teacher, was popular with the students.

But Florence Rouse had the ear of the principal, and the school board, not subject to appeal like other systems, supported his recommendation. It was therefore not surprising that the teachers were on tenterhooks, and submitted sullenly to being browbeaten. Malcolm's long history at St Edmund's, his popularity with the principal, and his docile acceptance of directives, therefore worked in his favour.

No one was sure where Florence had come from. She had entered the school at the beginning of the year like a bull in a china shop, with no attempt to immerse herself in the history or culture of the school, and no effort to consult with senior staff before implementing dramatic changes. Her initial attempts at friendliness only lasted a day or two as staff found her 'hale fellow well met' backslapping approaches, and her dictatorial style, overbearing. Little was known of her personal life, though the prefix of 'Miss' attached to her name on the school board in the foyer suggested that she lived alone. No teacher dared to mention the equivalent epithet they jokingly applied to Malcolm, 'Rouse by name and...' After all, schools have ears.

*

Ted Burkenshaw was the only teacher who had been at St Edmund's longer than Malcolm. He had recently made a few small errors in recording assessments that had been queried by parents, and he missed a half-yearly evening prize giving, thinking it was a day later. He had become a little forgetful in class, but he still taught well, the students were fond of him, and rather than bait him, they made allowances. At sixty-nine, he had less than a year to complete a notable career, and to be farewelled with the appropriate accolades.

Florence had other ideas.

'She's given me to the end of term,' Ted lamented. 'It's going to the board to be ratified next week, and that, as we all know, is a rubber stamp.'

Malcolm was outraged. 'But how can she do that? She has to know that you've given long and faithful service to St Edmund's. Have you been to Pennyworth?'

Ted, growing more disconsolate, shrugged. 'We both know what he'll say now that Rouse is calling the tune.'

They sat in silence for a minute.

'What does it mean for your pay-out?' Malcolm asked.

Again Ted shrugged. 'I don't know, but there'll be no going out in a blaze of glory for me,' and he left the room slowly as if the weight of the world was on his shoulders.

While it is not legal for staff to have access to the private information of others, Malcolm was able to obtain Florence's address from confidential staff files when the school clerk was taking dictation in the office. That night, having already debated for hours the wisdom of his proposed intervention, he knocked on the door of her unit, believing that his plea might have more impact away from her throne, her seat of power.

He was naturally anxious that he would receive a hostile reception, but he found her surprisingly convivial.

'I know it's no social call, Meek,' she smirked, 'and you don't have to be Einstein to guess why you've come. So before you start, the answer is no.'

Malcolm was not deterred. 'If he had five years to go,' he began,

'I could understand, but he's only months away from retirement. He's done more for the school than anyone, and it seems cruel for him to go out under a cloud.' He left his trump card to the end. 'I'm happy to proof all his assessments and reports, sit in on his parent interviews, be his keeper more or less.'

'The man is incompetent, Meek,' she still maintained her resolution with no hint of compassion, 'and there's no place for him at a school like St Edmund's. The parents expect the best and deserve the best. I don't like you questioning my judgement, but I suppose you only do so out of loyalty to a friend, even if it is misguided loyalty. Now I have more important matters to deal with.'

That was his signal to leave. 'More important than a man's future,' Malcolm persisted.

'More important than Burkenshaw's future,' she answered stonily. 'For instance, the principal has entrusted me with the task of finding the person who stole the television,' she boasted. 'And that's no small undertaking.'

'That's easy,' Malcolm said defiantly. 'I stole it.'

For once, Florence seemed lost for words, but not for long. 'You stole it! You stole it,' she repeated, as if the realisation needed emphasis to become real. 'Are you serious? How dare you,' she almost spat. 'You do know it's a criminal offence?'

'I've served that school for twenty years, given my life to it, and what do I have to show for it? I might even give it to Burkenshaw as a farewell present.'

It didn't sound at all like the Meek that Florence knew.

'I need a drink,' he continued, and taking in the room at a glance, strode to a cabinet, opened it and took out a decanter of whisky, half filling a glass and swallowing it in a single gulp.

Florence watched in disbelief.

'I should have offered it first to the lady,' he giggled, already seemingly affected. 'I don't suppose you have something to smoke,' he asked.

'I gave up cigarettes years ago,' said Florence, who, at first uncertain with this unpredictable change, resumed her more bellicose stance.

'I don't mean bloody cigarettes,' Malcolm shouted. 'I mean the hard stuff. Some weed, or whatever it is, that powder stuff you sniff.'

'I never have! How dare you,' Florence screamed, as Malcolm, ignoring the glass, took a swig from the decanter. 'You mean, you...' she was keen now to gather ammunition.

'Of course I do. What do you think keeps me going at that dumb school?' His words were becoming increasingly slurred.

'Just wait till the principal finds out about this,' Florence hissed with perverted satisfaction. 'Perhaps you can join your mate at the end of term, though I imagine in your case, it will be a lot sooner.'

'Well, you just go and tell the silly old goat,' Malcolm countered. 'Make sure you tell him what day of the week it is, and check that he's tied his shoelaces.'

'Get out,' she roared.

*

While he was sitting at his desk the next morning, Florence strode past him with a look of undisguised delight to the principal's office, a room adjoining the staffroom. The teachers, waiting at their desks for the first bell, exchanged questioning looks. All was eerily silent for the first couple of minutes, but then voices were raised. The barely audible monotone of Pennyworth's voice was drowned by Florence's voice that gradually increased in volume to become shouting. It continued unabated. The staff listened, trying to catch the drift. They could see Florence through the window, standing and wildly gesticulating. One of the junior teachers crept closer to the wall, but couldn't make out what was being said. Then suddenly the shouting stopped, the bell rang, and Florence emerged red-faced and sweating, to march from the staffroom staring fixedly ahead.

That afternoon, when Malcolm had a free period, he was called to the principal's office.

'Sit down, Malcolm,' Pennyworth said softly. 'Please accept my word that this is a delicate matter. I don't want to pry,' he began, 'but could you tell me what you did last night.'

'Certainly,' Malcolm replied. 'I stayed here to mark year nine's essays on the siege of Troy till about five o'clock, went home and took Rufus, my dog, on his usual walk to Bogonia Park, returned home, fed him and myself, sausages and mash for both of us, had a productive night writing a page of my book, and went to bed early, at about nine-thirty. Why do you ask?'

Pennyworth was quiet for half a minute, seeming to mull over what he should reveal. He stood, moved across to the window and pulled the blind, though no one was in the staffroom to observe. It created the aura of confidentiality he sought. 'I'm afraid Florence Rouse is having a breakdown. She was in here this morning carrying on like a banshee, saying the most ridiculous things. It set a very poor example for the staff. I'm well aware that they were listening, but enough of that. Our main concern must be for Miss Rouse. Dr Snell is coming in later this afternoon to give an opinion, and fortunately the school counsellor was on the premises this morning.'

'You're right,' Malcolm was all compassion. 'We are a family of sorts, and we need…' but before he had time to finish, Florence charged into the room, knocking a paperweight off the principal's desk.

'Tell him!' She faced Malcolm menacingly. 'Go on, tell him,' she shrieked. 'You stole the television, you reckon the school owes you, you're going to give it to Burkenshaw.'

Malcolm didn't respond, shaking his head, adopting silence as the best defence to counter such a tirade. Pennyworth raised his arms in supplication and subsided.

'You drink like a fish, and you're a drug addict,' she continued shouting. 'That's what keeps you going, you said. Tell the principal about your alcohol and drug addiction, Meek. The parents will be interested to find that their children are being taught by a drug addict at St Edmund's.'

'I told you what he called you, Mr Pennyworth.' She turned her attention to the principal, but she was becoming more hysterical. 'What was it, Meek?' She grabbed him by the shoulder.

Pennyworth started to rise, but eased himself down again as Florence released her grip.

'Old fool, or was it old goat, and he said you wouldn't know what day of the week it was. Liar,' she faced Malcolm. 'Liar.'

At that stage, Dr Snell arrived with an attendant, and they bustled a struggling Florence out of the room, still shrieking.

*

As the teachers left for their homes that afternoon, bewildered by the events of the day, Malcolm sat alone in the staffroom with Burkenshaw.

'What do you think that was all about, Malcolm?' Ted asked. 'We're all hearing different things about Rouse.'

'I'm as much in the dark as you are,' Malcolm replied, and patted his friend on the arm as he rose to leave. 'But with a bit of luck you might see out your time here, get that big farewell you deserve.'

For the first time in years, Malcolm ran with Rufus in the park, much to the dog's tail wagging delight. 'We may have to wait a while, old feller,' he told Rufus, walking more sedately on the way home, 'but in a month or two we might be able to watch a brand-new television.'

Spencer

We started school together, and as near-neighbours caught the same green and cream bus that wheezed its way up hills and around tight bends to shudder to a stop at the local primary school. We played the obligatory games of marbles, sharing our spoils, collected cigarette cards and matchbox toys, swapped conversation lollies with our favoured girls, and were both flautists in the school band, driven to community celebrations by one of our mothers, dressed in our navy wool shorts, white shirts, tartan sashes and navy school-crested caps, to be lauded by dignitaries, smiling benignly and espousing specious optimism about the future of the next generation.

We were Cubs together, supplementing the virtues of reverence and cleanliness with those of community service and honest toil through our annual 'bob a job' responsibilities, and we played in both his and my cubby house at weekends when I wasn't required to help my father in the garden, and he wasn't forced to practise the piano.

Our parents played bridge each Friday night, and our families shared holiday slide showings from a temperamental 35-millimetre projector, evenings that left Spencer and myself comatose. We sometimes went for picnics together in the country, or outings to the beach. There wasn't much that Spencer and I didn't do together.

The rules in those days were incontestable, particularly those at school, and beyond the ken of children like us, so we rarely questioned them, never made a fuss – though, unlike my own inflexible faith in adult infallibility, Spencer often suffered a stroke of the cane for his irrelevant inquiries.

Perhaps it is the way of all children to fashion friendship for their own different ends, like the cubby house games that shift direction as each player takes a turn in assuming control over the action. And yet I imagine that Spencer's ends and mine were not dissimilar. We didn't fight, probably because our disagreements were rare and never intense enough to be divisive.

Spencer's family moved to the other side of Sydney when I entered high school, and I don't remember being saddened by the change. Perhaps it was the unemotional and contractual nature of our relationship, or it may have been that other passions seized my pubertal years, made more urgent claims, and lead to more committed liaisons.

Those schoolboy years were hedged by prescribed behaviours and moral certainties, though Spencer and I were not aware of that. It was simply the way things were. Even now, I don't think of freedoms won or lost. The soul of culture changes through the years, and every generation has its own rites of passage, its own inimitable costs.

*

It was a decade later before I met Spencer again. A girlfriend had heard of a comedy evening held each Friday night in a small theatre restaurant in Newtown. Each week, would-be comedians performed on a stage through a haze of cigarette smoke that thickened the dim lighting a shade of bluey grey. Leggy girls in short skirts took orders for wine between acts, and brought pretzels or cheese and biscuits.

The MC started with jokes, but when they were greeted by stony silence, he retreated to simple introductions with sham enthusiasm. There was a sameness about all the acts, the raffish dress, the nonchalant swagger onto the stage, the studied informality of the patter, the 'on my way here tonight' audience engagement, the mock self-denigration, and the pervasive sexual theme. While my girlfriend laughed, I could barely raise a smile.

'Our final act is a real favourite, a regular of ours and a great crowd-pleaser.'

The leggy girls retreated. Near empty drinks were quaffed.

'Give it up for Seymour Sloane.'

He entered like all the others with a studied lack of panache, and in jeans strategically torn around the knees. He tossed back the long and greasy hair that covered his forehead and eyes, and waved the hand-held microphone like a baton. The audience was captive now, minds agog to laugh. He strutted the stage reading his audience like a script, the full throated laughter from the predisposed, the prudish women thrilling to his bawdiness, the puzzled and hard of hearing needing irony explained, and even the rare hyena laugh that fed the hilarity.

Memory often precedes knowing, but eventually the nagging familiarity became knowledge. It was Spencer, a taller, fuller and still faithful if older version of my youthful playmate. But why Seymour Sloane, a name that might have been taken from a Raymond Chandler crime novel.

Leaving my girlfriend to chat with friends she'd met by chance, I was able to gain access to a small dressing room at the back of the theatre, and found him sitting in front of a full wall mirror bordered by dimly lit naked globes. Crumpled tissues opened on the dressing table like muddied flowers.

'Hi,' he said, seeing me behind him in the mirror and not turning.

I remained standing in the doorway. This was his patch. It was for him to make the first move.

'It's been a long while,' I offered lamely.

'Yes,' he replied, 'a lot of water under the bridge,' and tossing a few things into a bag, 'Sorry, but I have to fly. Nice to see you again, though.' And that was it.

For several months after that, he played a major part in Agatha Christie's *The Mouse Trap* at a local theatre. I saw him perform, and very competently, and while I left a message with the doorman that I would like to see him, it was never answered. After that, he seemed to disappear.

*

Three years later, my wife and I attended the opening of an exhibition of French impressionists at the NSW Art Gallery. It was for members only, and therefore by invitation. Champagne and petits fours were offered by professional waitresses before the director of the gallery delivered a brief introduction to the genre and the paintings.

'Look,' my wife nudged me and whispered, 'it's Raelene Divine.'

Raelene was one of Australia's top models, touted as a super model, a term that supposedly placed her in an exclusive league. She had received a lot of press lately for an ugly split with her American rapper boyfriend, and was dressed in a three-quarter-length skintight silver gown that hugged her body and accentuated her breasts and buttocks. Onyx earrings hung low beside her neck, and a black pendant dallied with her cleavage. Her entry caused a stir that was momentarily off-putting for the director, but after nodding in her direction, he continued.

Briefly diverted, everyone's attention returned to the talk. Everyone's that is except mine, for beside Raelene, arm-in-arm with her, resplendent in a light grey lamé suit, black silk shirt and expensive Italian shoes, looking tanned and meticulously groomed, was Spencer, or was it Seymour.

When the talk had finished, we were treated to a viewing of the paintings, and as my wife was anxious to hear the brief commentary on each of them, I couldn't easily get away. For a few minutes, I could see Spencer and Raelene at the back of the throng, or being taken aside by eager photographers. They were still clinging to each other. But when I eventually found an opportunity to make contact with Spencer, they had already left.

I felt deflated, and did a quick reconnoitre of the gallery. Security confirmed their departure. Was it possible that he hadn't seen me? It was obvious that their appearance at the gallery had little to do with a fascination for French impressionism. And if he had seen me, wasn't our history worth at least an acknowledgement, a few words or even a wave?

*

Michael and I were both thirty when he finally decided to get married. We were the best of friends, having met at university and pursued the same career, so it wasn't surprising that I was to be the best man. Apart from my responsibilities at the wedding, my customary role was to organise the buck's night. Michael and I are probably more staid than most of our friends, and while he initially resisted the idea of any further celebration, the wishes of the others prevailed.

We ate at a restaurant in the city, and our friends, claiming that the night was still young, and that the occasion warranted letting your hair down, pooled their limited knowledge of nightclubs at Kings Cross. Even they were hesitant about entering some places where scantily clad women, smiling from red glossy lips, stood enticingly at the door, or where signs with lurid pictures extolled the merits of strippers with names like Angel.

We found ourselves in a crowded bar and ordered drinks, watching the melange of people, the conventional couples in suits returning from the theatre, the single women flaunting their availability, the gay men, and the sad drunks.

I was fascinated by a woman leaning against the bar, and dressed in a short, red, body-hugging dress with puffed sleeves, and high, black platform shoes. Her hair was a cascade of dark chocolate ringlets below her shoulders, and her eyes were heavily caked with black make-up. She was no mere girl, but she had shapely legs and a good figure.

'How you doing, Chantelle?' a man called to her from the near end of the bar, and she turned to smile.

Could it be? She saw me, and I'm quite sure that for a second or two there was a look of recognition before she turned away. I excused myself to confirm my suspicions, and approached her at the bar, ignoring the whistling and 'she's not your type' teasing of my friends.

'Spencer,' I whispered to a turned back.

'It's Chantelle,' he said, turning round to face me and also whispering, 'And how are you? I'd heard you were married.'

I always thought myself to be a good conversationalist, but what could I say? The typical life journeys are more predictable scenarios, more amenable to the usual clichéd questions. 'Perhaps we could meet,' I offered.

He hesitated for a moment, looking a little uncomfortable, and before he could reply, a man dressed in black, adorned with heavy gold chains, took him by the arm, and giving me what could only be a warning look, led Chantelle away. My friends were quiet when I returned to the table, sensing that something unusual, something deeply personal had transpired.

For several years, a number of stories surfaced about Spencer. He certainly lived for some time in the escapist hippie subculture at Nimbin in NSW, sometimes dubbed the cannabis capital of Australia, and where sexual norms are very relaxed. The other reports are less certain. One had him living a life of mendicancy with Buddhist monks somewhere in south-east Asia, and being fed by locals because the order is not permitted to ask for anything. Another account had him teaching transcendental meditation in India. It was some time before I would hear of him again.

*

The message that he had returned home to die reached me from my mother, who had still kept in contact with his aged parents. Terminal cancer. I never found out what type. He'd love to see you, the message from my mother reported, and even now I'm not sure whether it was his wish or his parents'.

As I entered his sparsely decorated bedroom with its faded jungle-theme wallpaper and olive-green curtains, no doubt the unaltered legacy of his teenage years, I wondered for just a moment if this was another guise he was presenting to an unsuspecting world. Yet one look at him lying in that steel-framed bed was enough to confirm his illness. His face was bone-white and gaunt, and his body, vaguely outlined beneath the sheet, seemed shrunken. I found myself looking for a trace of Seymour, Chantelle or the art gallery sophisticate. There was none. Nor was there evidence of the Spencer I'd known as a boy.

'I don't know who I am,' he whispered hoarsely as if he'd anticipated the question I'd been pondering for half a lifetime. No 'hello'. It was the first thing he said. 'I don't suppose you've ever looked in the mirror and asked yourself who was looking back at you.' He coughed for several seconds, and a small line of blood appeared in the crease at the side of his mouth. 'I have. I'd look and look and look, and ask myself what that face revealed of me, what it meant, how it defined me.' His voice trailed away, and he grimaced. 'Or how I defined it.'

We sat in silence for a few minutes before he drifted into a restless sleep. It somehow hadn't been appropriate to start revisiting our childhood adventures, no time to tease sentiment, or recall emotion that never existed. I kept thinking about my first meeting with Seymour Sloane, and of how actors tell impresarios that they can play any role at any time, be anything the action demands, for they are several different people. Perhaps Seymour or Spencer was unable to interpret his one inherent script, but could only glory in his major role triumphs like a chameleon that changes its colour to disguise.

As he slept, I peered from the window at a grove of dense, interlocking shrubs in the backyard that formed what could well have been a submarine, a spaceship and a pirate's cave, at least in the fertile minds of infant boys. I wonder if Spencer ever felt the same when he moved here. We all play our parts, I thought, small children with their prompted lines, adolescents aping the roles of their idols, celebrities affecting to assume the world, all looking for a singularity of self, a oneness that some like Spencer will never find, and others, the Hamlets and Othellos, will only grasp when life's action is about to end.

Perhaps death will reveal the real Spencer, swab away the layers of pretence that have masked his face like theatre make-up. Might he have already called for a mirror to detect an emerging self? I have no wish to find out.

Unity

It's early morning, and as the dew retires from winking silver, and the sun climbs in the sky, he picks his way past hawthorn, along the winding path that's been beaten flat by centuries of feet. The golden symmetry of buttercups and bluebells stipple verdant green, and the scented air is alive with birdsong.

He reaches a tumbledown fence of stones that divides two lush fields by an ancient kissing gate, but being alone, is unable to fulfil its licence, and fancy, he muses, is a lame alternative. Climbing across, he avoids the steaming pats of horse's dung, and the dun-nosed sheep that stare foolishly.

Crossing a stile, he stops, breathing in the efflorescence of the English countryside. The ripened hills roll down in grassy tussocks, and he looks down on the striated fields that meet the ancient houses sleeping in the town. The silence, only enlivened by the blackbird's song, settles like a quilt and mutes the bleating of the sheep.

He sits on a freshly sawn tree stump feeling a relief he battles even then to explain to himself, a feeling of being somehow naked in this rarefied air, stripped of past and future, outside time, sanctified by this cathedral of the natural world, a part of it with the sheep, and the bees that grow languid on the hollyhocks.

Then some primal feeling makes him stand, and finding a flat piece of ground nearby, he lies down, supine among the smell and rub of coaxing grass, stretching out his arms and legs in dog-rich ease, and looking up at a pastel sky of gentle blue that's seamed with threads of cloud. His whole world seems to be opening anew with the springtime flowers, his pressures evaporating in the morning's thawing dew.

He can't remember how long he lay there, looking at the sky. His shirt was damp, clinging to a sore back, and his face was pink, warmed by the brightening sun. Is this where I belong, he asked himself, supine for all eternity, gazing at the sun and moon and stars, as grass and creeper entwine me, and the saplings root me to the earth in welcome anonymity?

*

Colin Smith saw himself as an ordinary sort of man. Even his name didn't seem to confer distinction. Reared in a modest middle-class suburb in Sydney with a mixture of new and older liver-brick houses, he went to good schools, was an above average student, and was well liked by his peers. His initial public service job, that he'd never left, followed an unremarkable university education. The work was routine rather than absorbing, but it gave security, four weeks annual holiday, and good superannuation.

In his early fifties, he'd retained his youthful figure, kept the hint of developing softness around his middle well disguised, and combed the long thin wisps of light brown thinning hair so that they covered his creeping baldness. He was fastidious in his dress, and some called him handsome.

The failure of his marriage might also be regarded as ordinary, at least in the statistical sense, but its impact, while softened by his two children, who had remained attentive to his needs, left a deep scar. He'd married young, nursing a doubt that this feeling for Anne was as good as it gets. They had a lot in common, returned insights like ping-pong balls, and completed each other's sentences. They laughed and cried together. The absence of romantic love as he'd once known it was challenged by the tug of imminent sex that proved particularly seductive for the uninitiated Colin, and by the constant warnings he received from parents and older friends about the capricious nature of romance. 'It doesn't last' was the mantra.

The marriage's decline was formulaic, the disappointment from unmet expectations, and the resentment leading to the breakdown of communication.

'Why can't you talk to me?' she'd plead. 'Why can't you say what you feel?'

'I've tried,' he'd retort. 'So many times I've tried. You don't seem to understand.'

And so, in those last months, the intimacy disappeared. He'd lie next to her, supine in the marital bed, and sense, almost hear, her mind at work, the wheels turning, before she'd turn out the bedside lamp and turn her back to him. Then after wordless breakfasts, he'd kiss her cheek and leave for work as fractious children searched for homework, squabbling to the car.

He remembers the pain of those first years on his own, waking in his rented unit to the winter's grey and feathery sky that always seemed to weigh too much, hearing the mournful crows lament another day, and having to brave the reassuring platitudes and hollow voices from their underwater caves.

Occasionally he would call to mind the brief and innocent romantic relationship he'd known before he'd met Anne, when the clichés about the world standing still all rang true. He'd conjure those moments when he was alone in the natural world, watching the silver plate of moon from a cliff top, or walking barefoot along a sunny beach, to test his loss with bitter-sweet desire. He thought of seeing her again, perhaps a little coarsened by an ample life, her puzzled look before recall, and the comic revelation of their private narrative to entertain a husband's playfulness. Instead, he decided to keep his grand illusion intact, believing a suspect martyrdom to be safer than an unknown reality.

In later years, whenever he contemplated the end of his marriage, his thoughts were recast by each successive revisiting. What interpretation might he provide now to the interrogator wanting to know why it failed? How different would it be to that of years ago? At the time, Anne had demonised him. By making him the villain, the dragon, she was the dragon-slayer, the heroine. Would she feel any different now?

The years passed, and Colin bought his own unit, spent time with his children, who had both left the family home where they had remained with their mother, and devoted himself to work. He joined a bushwalking club, attended a series of history courses conducted by the University of the Third Age, and renewed his interest in running. He saw different women occasionally, but these contacts were brief skirmishes more than relationships.

So where to from now, he wondered. His intellect told him he was not alone, no more so than most people, yet he felt alone, sometimes despairingly so. Retirement was not that far away, and what had he achieved? What could he boast? What legacy could he leave? Yes, he was an ordinary man. He recalled the words about the 'uses' of the world spoken by Hamlet, 'weary, stale, flat and unprofitable', and wondered about the purpose of it all, a short time slaving on earth, trying to do your best, and then nothing. The finality was appalling.

*

Mayfield is a large and quaint village in the north-east of Sussex, nine miles south of Tunbridge Wells. Its village sign depicts a young woman with children in a flowered meadow, indicating the Saxon origins of the village's name, Maghefeld or 'Maid's Field'.

It's here that Colin arrived in the English spring, immediately impressed after leaving the bus, and wearied from an interminable and cramped flight, wheeling his luggage for a fortnight's visit to his only cousin, walking down the high street with its attractive raised red-brick pavements, and past Middle House, a grand oak-beamed Tudor inn.

'It'll do you good,' his family encouraged.

'Something new and different,' his friends insisted. 'You need an adventure.'

It wasn't something he'd considered, but his plans changed when he received an invitation from the cousin, years older than himself and busy in his senior years when mortality makes its more pressing claims, researching his ancient and more immediate origins.

The cousin and his wife were the perfect hosts, indulging him, yet giving him the freedom for time to himself that they intuited he needed. For the cousin, it was an intellectual response to things said or not said; for his wife, it was empathy.

'He's such a nice fellow,' she said to her husband in their usual daily reckoning, their hands locked in bed that first night, 'and I get the sense that he's searching for something.'

The house was comfortable, set among flowering shrubs, and with a short walk to the high street. He was given a spacious room that belonged to one of their long departed children.

It was the morning after his arrival that he'd left a note on the kitchen bench and had taken his first of many solitary walks, intending to return before breakfast.

'Whatever have you been up to?' the cousin's wife laughed when he entered hours later with his shirt damp and coloured with a faint green tinge, and a leaf pressed to its sleeve.

*

St Dunstan's is an ancient and imposing church set back from the high street, rebuilt after being destroyed by fire in 1389, and rumoured to once have been the residence of several mediaeval Archbishops of Canterbury. Colin had always enjoyed visiting churches, particularly those steeped in history, as they gave him a great sense of calm and serenity.

Although only mid-afternoon, the sun was already a peachy residue settling on the bottom of the sky. The rising walls of lichened sandstone, etched in silhouette were stark against the sky. He walked around the church and was surprised to find the acres of graves, chastening reminders of the dead that subdued him with certain prophecy. They were upright and askew, or broken and lying face down, some with bold inscriptions, or prideful with a wilting rose, still exerting a claim on life; and others were smoothed by needling rain and bare with lost posterity.

Colin moved slowly and reverentially around the graves, and if they were not enclosed by rusted metal railings, or hemmed by stone, was careful not to tread on the faces of the dead. He read the epitaphs, or rather let them speak to him, but they revealed little from their miserly chronologies.

He saw her kneeling by a grave on the other side of the cemetery, neatening a plot with a small spade, trowel and clippers, a curious sight, he thought, his mind full of village legends and the stories of witches that pillage graves at night. She'd seen him and waved, so even though forever shy, he felt able to approach.

'Leah,' she greeted him, standing and extending her fine-boned hand with unsophisticated style. In her forties, her baggy pants and old woollen jumper couldn't hide her figure, or detract from the prettiness of a peaches and cream English complexion, an aquiline face and pale blue eyes. She was remarkably clean despite her labours, except for a smudge of dirt on her cheek that he was sorely tempted to remove with his handkerchief.

'He's not a relative,' she explained, nodding towards her work. 'As you can see, Rupert Tanner has been dead a good while. The choking weeds and crumbling stone need care, and I think the dead deserve respect. So I come here twice a week and spend a few hours tidying up. You can see what I've done,' and she pointed towards the church where the graves and surrounds were neat. 'Besides,' she added as an afterthought, 'it's just so peaceful here.' And she knelt down and resumed her work.

Colin asked if he could help and knelt beside her, helping her secure the stone tablet in an upright position, and taking the trowel to follow her lead. They chatted as the darkness spread, and the sun slanted between the majestic towers of the church. The talk carried an honesty and intimacy that Colin had not known for years. He'd later wonder if it was the chemistry between them, or the audience of knowing dead, for who, he asked himself, could better appraise the slings and arrows that we bear, than those who've lived it all before?

A slight wind was whispering round the towering stone of the church, recycling and chilling to the bone.

'I really have to go,' she said reluctantly. Colin helped her stand, gathered her tools, and for a moment she hesitated, holding rather than shaking his hand.

He watched her till she disappeared, and lingered in the frozen night, bare of stars, sitting on a tombstone, and feeling no urgency to leave.

'I don't think Albert Winthrop would mind,' he told himself. 'Nor would the village postman smarting with his Great War wounds, the little girl who never knew the secrets of her sex, or Ethel Cavendish at ninety-three who is still guarding the church she once adorned with flowers.' He'd never felt this way before, this unity of the natural world and humankind, the peace of life and death in harmony.

Catalyst

A boy of mid-teenage years approaches, one flap of his shirt awry, pulled from his trousers by a simian gait, or by the constant swaying that he can't control. But he manages to move forward, even with the leg that capers like a hose that isn't held.

He's one of a number of physically and intellectually challenged adolescents and adults of indeterminate age who come here regularly on a community bus. Those with Down's syndrome are often taken to the small kiosk for morning tea. Those with more serious impairments usually occupy one of the pergolas or sit on the lawn where their carers provide morning tea from a Thermos.

Lake Parramatta is a picturesque place. Gum trees, statuesque and painterly, climb from the water's rocky bank, and in season the furry wattle hijacks the sun and bends like mellow fruit across the sunlit olive of the lake.

Many of these visitors appear indifferent to the ducks that glide in gleaming phalanx, or the sulphur-crested cockatoos swooping between the towering gums. Perhaps it's hard for anyone to articulate what they really see, or to express their feelings about the luminescing blues and sun-shot yellows, or to fathom what lies behind the blue unblemished sky and the mirrored lake, enigmas of concealment and disguise.

'You're staring,' he admonishes, turning his eyes away from the approaching boy, unwrapping the peanut slice and hoping that he didn't sound critical. He's suddenly aware of his steady hands, and the fingers that flex and work together as he serves the slice.

'And of course you're not,' she answers with a gentle touché, disguising her irritation. She was after all busy pouring the coffee. There's always something wrong, she thinks, with nearly everything I say or do. It seemed like a good idea to come at the time. It used to be one of their favourite haunts. Now being here seems to be at odds with the separation that she bitterly regrets. The pain is bad enough. Better to say nothing, to let the tension drain in these idyllic surroundings, and perhaps in time to restore something of what they used to have.

*

When they first began a relationship two years ago, he'd been attracted by her innocence, her femininity and her lack of worldliness. She had an ingenuous quality that conferred vulnerability, something that his masculinity found very appealing.

The usual perfunctory chatter at a party, the typical formula for introductions between strangers, deepened into something more meaningful as empathy revealed itself, and chemistry worked its magic. There was no anxiety for either of them in arranging a rendezvous. It was a seamless addition to that first conversation, a shared expectation. Until he saw her again, he kept thinking of her large brown eyes, the shoulder-length blonde hair with its scent of roses, and the hint of caution in her smile, perhaps a fear of letting go.

Their first meeting was at Lake Parramatta, a place to which they'd often return, a place that became a sentimental retreat and a sacred canvas for both of them. And as romance tightened its hold, so did the aphrodisiac of talk and touch. By the time they left, the shadows were creeping across the grass, and a tangerine sun hung low on the lake. The incremental give and take, the dance of love, edged towards intimacy, though he was careful not to push too hard. He surprised himself by not wanting to do so, and found her restraint a compliment, a statement of how she perceived her worth. Her tenderness was captivating.

'Kindness', 'consideration', 'caring', 'compassion', this was the cluster of like-meaning words he'd use to describe her to his friends. She worried, often needlessly about the well-being of her family, she sent cards and letters of reassurance to people she hardly knew who'd fallen on hard times, she surprised him and others with gifts that she could barely afford, sacrificed her time when others sought her comfort. And continued to do these things when the favour was not returned.

Because her kindness shone, and never sought to gain, he felt the gods had smiled on him, and loved her more. But such an expansive spirit often comes at a cost. At work, envy and jealousy would often be expressed in clandestine bitchiness, by small minds united in the sharing of their common impotence. Even her sisters were guilty of the odd barbed comment.

'You know what people are most envious of? What they really can't swallow?' The question he put to a group of friends was rhetorical. 'It's not money, or power or status, achievements or good looks. It's goodness. Simple goodness. People can't cope with that because they're all too aware of their own shortcomings, or the darkness that lurks inside them. It can't be bought. It's non-negotiable and enduring.'

Yet gradually this goodness palled, even for him. He thought she could be more discerning, that she was sometimes naive in giving to others all the time, and getting little in return. She didn't seem to understand that the more she gave, the more people expected her to continue doing so. Her very goodness, or what he began to see as her naivety or her own need, became a stick that was all too frequently used to beat her with.

He began to question the virtue of placing others' needs above your own. He had always regarded himself as 'a giver', as someone who was more sensitive than most to the needs and moods of others. He certainly saw the need for some self-sacrifice for other people's benefit, but surely putting others first all the time was seeing oneself as less worthy. It was giving to others because they deserved it more.

At first, he explained this to her, and while she listened, and saw the wisdom of what he said, nothing seemed to change. It wasn't just the unrequited charity, or the refusal to retaliate when someone had been unconscionably unkind. It was her idealism, her unlimited faith in humankind, her vision of a gracious community like Prospero's happy isles. And so his subtle censure sidled to reproach.

'I know you think I'm being silly,' she'd say. 'I know you think I don't understand what people are really like, but I do. This is who I am. Perhaps the world would be a better place…' And his criticism of her unworldliness would collapse before her nobility, at least for a while. But as the months rolled by, his criticisms gained an edge, particularly when she kept being hurt.

There were times when he felt that he had been unkind, and was contrite. He never doubted his love for her, and sometimes wondered if he harboured some resentment, if her goodness was something he couldn't achieve, a challenge he couldn't match. At times he was more philosophical and saw the conflict as an inevitable part of what it means to love someone, that while love may carry us to thrilling virgin worlds, we battle to sustain its frail nobility before it plunges to a petty depth of imagined affront. Perhaps, he told himself in more serene moments, a love that's weathered in such a fire emerges from these challenges like tempered steel to offer something even more real.

But his disappointment with the selfishness or meanness of those who took her for granted, or who hurt her, increasingly became directed at her entrenched need to keep giving, and her refusal to stand up for herself when unjustly treated.

*

It was the tone of his voice. 'You're staring.' It was the heavy condemnation that had become typical this last half-year.

She had watched the boy for a few seconds in the same way she might watch anyone heading towards them. She wasn't gawking. There was nothing untoward, nothing rude or morbid in her glance. Is that what he was implying?

This year she was teaching Billy at school, a boy whose head was exaggeratedly askew and whose body was cruelly twisted to upset a natural walk. His classmates couldn't do enough to help and always rose to his defence, the girls solicitous and sisterly, the boys more silent yet with tacit male concern, all fructifying in their teenage years beside Billy's antiseptic frailty. And she couldn't do enough for him, willing to rush to his defence, assume the rash crusade of youth to plead a cause. Children like Billy were nothing new for her.

She knew she wasn't worldly, that she didn't 'put it out there', but didn't see this as a minus. Nothing was more odious to her than female conceit. She wasn't confident and knew that her history of looking after younger brothers and sisters might have cemented her practice of giving service to others. But to expect her to change herself at this stage of her life was like asking the stars to fall out of the sky.

I'm a good person, she'd say, as if she needed the claim endorsed to make up for other shortcomings. And when she felt that she hadn't given enough, or later in the relationship when she felt she'd let him down, she was quick to condemn herself. 'I'm not a good person,' she'd say, to his amazement.

She'd had other boyfriends, but he was different. Lists of desirable qualities might give some evidence of attraction, but are generally invalid. They are only post hoc proof of feeling. He was attentive. He was sensitive, empathic, and seemed to understand her. He bought her small gifts of pendants, earrings and rings, and their timing was always perfect. But her love existed despite them. That feeling couldn't be reasoned.

She was painfully aware of his irritation with her for constantly turning the other cheek, and for continuing to give when such giving was never returned or in some way used against her. As his criticisms gained an edge, she did try to change her ways, but the resulting guilt over letting someone down made her miserable. And even though she agreed with him that it often left her disappointed and exhausted, she found his reaction difficult to understand, and sometimes felt annoyed with him. He was being very unfair. Didn't he want her to care for others? After all, he was the main apologist for considering others' needs. Yet wanting to appease, she gave him even more, the thousand small indulgences that only a partner can know.

Two months ago, they'd had a fiery exchange.

His mood was sour. 'Why don't you stand up and be counted?'

That day she had politely acquiesced to doing another staff member's work at her school, someone who shirked work at every opportunity with no thought for who it might inconvenience. And the day before, she had silently suffered an unfair criticism from her sister.

'Because it's who I am,' she said in defence. 'And if you don't like it…' She'd never been that confronting before, and even though there'd been no belligerence in her answer, she instantly regretted her last remark.

'I don't.' He was more blunt than usual. He spoke some harsh words that wounded her, but the contrition he might normally feel evaporated in the face of her silent acceptance.

They agreed to separate.

*

'Hello,' the boy rasps in a stentorian voice. His beanie is pulled down over his forehead to meet the deep-set eyes in a pinched but not unsightly face. 'I'm going for a walk.' The words are separate like beads counted on a string. His pride goes charging through the phlegmy drawl. He beams with pleasure, and flaps his hands.

'You enjoy your walk. It's a lovely day for it,' she encourages him, and is rewarded with a toothy smile that opens his face.

'Yes, I will. I will enjoy my walk,' the boy answers with the same emphasis, now full of importance.

They both watch him go, this time without reproaching each other. He stands, feeling the strength flowing through his limbs, intoxicated by his robustness, his spine so straight and his arms and legs, that spring unthinking, blooded into life. And for the first time, he feels uneasiness, something like a shame that's little tempered by relief at feeling whole. He stretches as though he is testing himself before he sits down again.

They drink their coffee and eat the peanut slice in silence, avoiding eye contact, and resisting the stock cliché about the grace of God, watching the ducks with sunflower yellow beaks, spread out in brilliant white, gliding with glistening wake, and the nameless bird life swooping and keening.

She moves from the pergola to sit in the shade of a towering gum that claws the rock near the glittering lake, welcomes the mental liberty the landscape is giving her. And in the reverent silence, she's surprised by the sudden awareness of his presence by her side, his hand very gently on her shoulder, a hand that carries the same palpable message of two years ago.

Home

Most of us return to thoughts of our childhood home, picking the memories clean like pilling on a vest, to times when all the world was home, a place you learned to eat and sleep and love, perhaps to die.

The abiding childhood images of family togetherness for many of us in my generation are the Sunday outings. For me, they were in the old Ford Prefect with the scent of chocolate from father's weekend surprise, chocolate my brother and I tried to leave unsucked on our tongues to make it last, chocolate that insinuated with the fragrance of my mother's lavender. Beyond the car's side window I'd initial with my breath, I'd watch the country hurtle by, all open vistas beneath a sky of softened blue that smiled on straw-coloured grass, and a random Jersey cow. At nine, I'd watch my father's long-lobed ears that hung beside the silver sprouting hairs around his neck, and feel strangely wakened to his fallibility, a feeling that became a tenderness for all the world, though a feeling I was too young to understand. And a feeling that disappeared when I left the car with its imposed complicities to squabble with my brother and question the arbitrariness of adult law.

Growing up, the weekends were peaceful eternities, and a time to play in the cubby house, an old wooden packing case for a car that stood beside the paling fence, lodged between privets. It was a ship, plane and rocket that carried its all-conquering superheroes to many hostile lands and returned them unscathed for mother's cups of tea and freshly baked biscuits.

The weekends were also a time that I had to work with my father in our unruly and constantly overgrown backyard, weeding the gardens, thrashing the clods of earth against the spade to separate both the weeds and the grubs that the magpies swooped on. I thought it an imposition at the time, and only as an adult wondered if it achieved any useful purpose, but began to understand that it was a strategy of my fathers to teach responsibility, and his opportunity for communion with his sons. The image of him leaving home at eight-fifteen a.m. in the Prefect with his suit and homburg hat remains a novelty for our hatless workers' generation.

On weekdays at six p.m., before the grind of homework, my brother and I would listen to the fifteen-minute radio serials before we improvised our own in bed later that night. We had no television in my early years. Superman was a great radio favourite, and a model for imagined 'show-off' rather than 'do-good' aspirations. Then after dinner, it was downstairs to the converted tool room where we both studied, my makeshift desk shelved with wooden fruit boxes, still labelled by suppliers, and in which I kept my texts and work books. Shut off from the other activities in the house, the only interruption was the whining plumbing from the exposed overhead pipes, or the scurrying of possums underneath the house.

My sequestered teenage years were daunting for a gentle boy who felt unvintaged like most of my contemporaries, and yet my mother understood that it was a time for introspection and discovery, and knew that dogged love, dished out like apple pie or sausage sandwiches for school, would in the end suffice. From my tiny room, a converted sun room beyond the kitchen door, a room in which I kept books gleaned from my father, harbouring insights yet unknown, I'd hear my mother in the kitchen next door at six a.m. preparing the porridge and setting out the breakfast things. It made little impression at the time, but I see it in retrospect as a symbol of security in those tumultuous maturing years. She'd later type my essays on the old Remington, and there was always a hot meal on the table when I returned home late from work or university. She never complained. I still sometimes wonder if servitude like hers is really friend or foe, yet who am I as grateful heir to arbitrate?

Of course, no family is a picture of harmony. There are always faint antipathies that crawl beneath the fabric of a cheerful family life. One was the silent protest of this youthful idealist at all his father might have done to repay his wife's illimitable service. Another was the competition, applauded by the generation of the times, between two sons only two years apart in age. We wrestled on the buffalo lawn, where we gave ourselves alliterative names of would-be champions, and played cricket in the backyard with a crudely fashioned paling bat that we used to guard both a fruit-box wicket, and our naked shins. We played table tennis on the back veranda, where I was compelled to hit down the line, because I was required to make the trek outside to retrieve my forehand winners. Winning was important, and disputes sometimes resulted in a temporary break from such activities.

There were also times of great harmony, like the Christmas dinners traditionally attended by the extended family, the exchanging of gifts, and a pudding secreting threepences. I have a Christmas photograph that looks like a gallery of rogues: one aunt, vanilla-scented and intent with a slow release of steam in intermittent laugh; the other aunt, more nonchalant, probably brooding on more animated scenes; her husband, bland and tumid-eyed behind thick lens; and Hilda, my grandmother, with eyes that nursed the world. They all look comical in ill-fitting paper hats unravelled from bonbons. And there were the nights of family parlour games when a creamy moon lodged in a pane, jasmine's heavy-scented breath was redolent, and there was a real togetherness.

Home was a place I experienced my first kiss when still at primary school, a quick and embarrassed peck on the lips from Susie, who lived a few doors away, a kiss that was followed a few days later with a written message: 'If you love me like I love you, only death can part us two.' At eleven, I didn't know how to respond, and did nothing.

'Address?' my teachers would ask in my early days at school, recording personal information, and so I'd parrot the number, street and suburb. I had been well drilled. There were no postcodes then, and phone numbers were recorded with letters as well as numbers. When my peers later asked where I lived, I didn't parry with 'abide' or 'thrive'.

There was no difference then, and yet it was a place you'd one day leave, with wistful parents at the door.

*

Returning once again after many years, I felt 'at home' yet somehow not, belonging yet remote, a servant of two different lives, the one I'm living now, and the one I was living then, tethered by a spare chronology.

The pearls hung looser round my mother's throat. Her years were heavy then, and I tried to close my mind and feelings to their raids on permanence, impatient with the skitter of her mind and hearing loss. It's not that I didn't care. I needed a scapegoat for my own sprinting years, and her failings were becoming my own bequest.

My father's denim eyes were vitreous. He was less robust and his voice had softened to a whisper. I think the passion and protest had been replaced by more sober reflection. That same morning he'd returned from his sister's funeral, and I needed no literacy to imagine the thoughts that flitted across the years as he listened to the eulogy, probably the typical bald chronology that leaves the departed fixed on a pin, like an exhibit with a technical Latin tag, revealing nothing of her blaze of love or her smell of fear. Even in his senior years, he would want to rip the words apart to expose her very essence, and confront the unction of the priest who dampened earthly sentiment, belittling self for promises of life beyond.

We all sat together on the porch, history and lineage conferring empathy. The tales I resurrected of childhood escapades seemed enervated by the years. 'Remember the time there was a misunderstanding about my staying over at Michael's, and you thought I was lost or had been abducted, and called the police?' They'd nod, and there was a hint of smiles. 'Or when Dane knocked over that can of paint on the hall carpet.' They nodded in concert.

The passionate talk of sport and politics had also been relegated to a grudging second place, and medical stories were shared that met with little reaction, perhaps a despondent shake of the head, and always trumped by limitless mortality: 'It's in all the organs now and terminal, a month or two at best, not forty yet, and three little kiddies under ten.' They both seemed inured to the inevitable.

I thought of the dialogue that was becoming all too common with my friends: the counting of liver spots, the devouring of caches of pills, the subscriptions purchased at gyms, and the waking in early morning hours to feel a tenderness that loiters deep inside waiting to pounce. And I began to understand what it was like for my mother and father.

'How are the children?' my father asked, and my mother put down her knitting to listen. 'Amity must be nearly twenty now. It's been such a long time since we've seen them.'

'From now on you'll be seeing them a lot,' I promised. 'Now that I'm back, we'll make regular visits.'

From the silence that beckoned their siesta on the porch, my father's first 'I love you' struggled from the thaw within, and I knew the evening meal my mother cooked would be good basic fare.

I stayed the night. My brother's room had become a study cum sewing room. My father still followed the stock market, and had the occasional flutter. My mother had taken to quilting, and several women came each week and worked together, sitting around a table where my brother's bed used to be. My own room was unchanged. Even the sporting trophies were still on the wall shelf, sparkling silver. The desk was beside the window from which I would look out on the luminous night sky, pierced, I thought, by meddling stars.

The ambivalence of feeling that I belonged, yet had moved on, was never greater than when I entered this room. And yet there was always great comfort there where roots entwined the bedrock of my ways. Something always drew me back till safety overwhelmed.

*

'I lived here once,' I tell the plump young woman tending the garden, needing to explain my curiosity, and the nostalgia that has brought me back. Her pride in what she has done overrides any alarm she might have felt, and she asks if I would like to look around.

I would have preferred the time to myself, to wander and linger, to indulge the images of what used to be, but understandably, I'm led from room to room, her tireless commentary deadening fond recall. 'We took out the wall here. It opens the place up, seems to let more light in. And a servery here means we don't have to walk around from the kitchen any more.'

The wall she talks about was where my brother and I put the dates and measured our heights. I can still remember the pencil marks against the door, and my standing on tiptoes, complaining that my mother didn't keep the ruler straight, because I wanted to tell the girls at school I was taller than I was. That wall also held the hook my father screwed in for the keys, a hook diverting us to lighter moods that left us grinning through the years, a reminder that my brother left his key there once, and neighbours called the police because they couldn't recognise him climbing in the window in the early hours. We roasted him for that every birthday.

The rooms seem to have shrunk in time, their mellowness replaced by garish hues, the furnishings all glass and chrome. My bedroom chrysalis where budding feelings simmered in a stew of imaginings, and where television in my later teenage years mocked my understanding of a dawning world, is now clad in boy-band prints, and hot-pink taffeta. A maroon fabric light with tassels hangs down to head height. Photos of singing idols outnumber school imperatives on a wall cork-board.

'Look what we've done with the main,' she says with relish, and in her enthusiasm she reaches out as if she is going to lead me by the hand. 'We put in those built-ins. Brett's thinking of taking out the wall here as well, making the room next door a walk-in robe.' It's my room she's talking about. 'The flocked wallpaper works, doesn't it?' she says.

The bed is facing a different way, yet despite the changes, the room is somehow still thick with meaning. My brother and I clambered on the bed in here to unwrap all the presents we were given. I picture my long-gone parents sitting up in bed and grinning at our childish enthusiasm.

Two girls rush past, dropping their school bags in the hall.

'So rude,' their mother laughs. 'At least say hello to our visitor.' She can't give a name. I never gave one.

'Hello,' one says cheerily.

'Hello, Mr Visitor,' the other says a little flirtatiously, and they both race to the kitchen, where I hear the fridge open and close, and the clinking of glasses.

I gratefully take my leave, noticing the metre-high garden gnome, garishly painted in reds and blues, standing guard on the front porch where my parents once sat together on the swing seat before their afternoon siesta. It is so ludicrous, I have to stop myself from laughing. I see my parents on the swing seat, both in their set place, my father with a novel, mother with her quilting. 'What is that strange thing?' my mother asks with an air of disapproval, stopping her quilting and nodding towards the gnome. ' I love you, son,' my father replies.

At the top of the ramp, I move across the street to my car, and don't look back. There's no sadness, no regrets. Even a buoyancy of sorts. All is as it should be. Most houses are only bricks and mortar, but it takes a lot of living for a house to be a home. I'm no Orpheus. My childhood home will never disappear.

Cuckold

He's suddenly aware as never before of the detail of the room, a sharpness of perception – the chocolate leather lounge that's dulled and creased where he always sits, the virtuosity of the Hugh Sawry brass of 'Waltzing Matilda' on the buffet, the beige carpet with the red wine stain that they concealed by moving the Sutherland table to cover it, and the tear in the heavy gold drapes they open each morning to welcome the morning sun.

Portent now gathers in the room where sunlight stipples the dusty windowpane, and where an unnatural calm settles, a suspension of time and thought that heralds momentous action, the legendary calm before the storm.

For him, something of great significance is greeted with an air of unreality, the endless imagining and rehearsing for an event that finally arrives, but does so with a feeling of unbelief. He walks slowly about the room, readying himself, testing his resolution now that the time has come. She is sitting in the single floral lounge chair, perhaps a little flushed, probably his imagination, with her hair tied back to reveal the delicate whiteness of her neck, a feature that has always appealed to his old-fashioned Edwardian sense of the romantic.

Yet because he feels the power is his – after all, he is the aggrieved one here – his hostility is tempered by a sympathy that he wrestles to overcome. Or is it the love for her that still holds him in its steady grip and that threatens to halt his challenge?

She feels cocooned by her listlessness, a foil to his agitation. She watches him pacing the room, fully aware of what is to come, reading it from the tightened lips, the furrowed brow and the stiffness in his tread that always precedes argument. She turns her eyes to the window that's opened a few centimetres to reveal the raiding slice of sun with its bouncing motes.

It doesn't seem to matter any more. She's lived this moment many times before in many different guises, sometimes in nightmare anguish, and at other times in more sober reflection. She even wonders what form of déjà vu the reality will take, what stance he might adopt. Will it be violence, hostility, reasonableness, pleading, perhaps nobility? But she won't dissemble. Lying might demean the only thing that's real.

*

He was even disconcerted by the old photos she showed him, picturing her sitting in another's lap, or nestling in the crook of another's arm, presuming a mutual ownership. For Brian, old photos had a sense of vanquished time, something exposed and irredeemable, and, for the particular photos he laughed about with Jane, a pervasive loss of innocence.

'Of course I'm jealous,' he told her light-heartedly, wondering what images were not caught, the privacy of bygone loves that resist recall.

'But they're years old,' she laughed, touched by his innocence.

His love had been immediate, the frisson of their first intoxicating words, the bursting feelings held in check before the dizzy certainty of safe return, and later, the unexpected gift of responsive bodies feeding in a locked embrace, the bond so tried and true that even their rare arguments renewed a tensile love.

His most endearing image was that of her at Kiama as he stood on the balcony of their resort room in the early morning, with the greedy sunlight even then running like honey in the room, and the plush of vintage green below, with the ocean mugging the sand in dull relentless growls. He felt so disarmed, and so aroused by a painful tenderness as he watched the innocence of her sleep inside.

So what went wrong? They'd been married for seven years. There'd been no 'itch' for him, but her loss of interest was all too apparent.

She no longer desired sex, and submitted with reluctance, not saying a word, and rolling over when it was finished. Her once strong interest in his work was now rare and superficial, and she found countless reasons to avoid going out with him.

'Your wife and Jim Ferrier are certainly hitting it off,' one of his friends told him at the club, watching him closely for his reaction.

That was the first suggestion that there might be someone else. Later that night, as a celebration raged inside, he retired to the balcony to see a couple separate from an embrace, and hurry inside from another door. It was dark, and he couldn't be sure, but Jane's gown was adorned with sequins, and the moon had picked out stars of silver in the dim light. Jane was laughing at a speech when he returned inside, but seemed self-conscious, and intent not to look in his direction.

Then there was the time he found a not-so-cryptic note in the dirty washing basket – '3 this arvo usual place' – when Jane had mentioned visiting her mother. He noticed their studied avoidance of each other at various social occasions, an exaggerated indifference, and the farewell brushing of hands. And there was the humiliation of people beginning to talk, the sympathetic looks from knowing women, and Jim's forced attempts at camaraderie.

He tried to give more, buying her little gifts, mainly sentimental tokens, offering to assume some of the tasks that become typed by gender or routine in marriage, and showing increased interest in her daily activities. But she viewed his sudden change with suspicion.

Tortured every day by fanciful images, he imagined the obscenity of Jim's flexed buttocks locked by Jane's glabrous thighs. He saw her stretching naked, feline on the bed and beckoning, or undressing provocatively as Jim watched, slowly peeling off those sheer stockings she'd never worn for him. Whenever she returned home, he looked for signs of her being dishevelled, or bearing the kippered scent of aftermath. Of course he might be mistaken. It might only be a flirtation that they'd managed to hold in check.

I'm a cuckold, he told himself, afraid to confide it even to the best of his friends. He consulted the dictionary: 'a man whose wife has committed adultery'. It seemed so matter-of-fact, so bald, with no Latin tags to lend it a shred of mystique or decency.

*

In the mangle of the years, Jane's amorous feeling for Brian had been squeezed of love's nectar and rolled dry. She often felt bemused by what had once enchanted and aroused her, what alchemy had united them to share their dreams years ago. And while she was anxious about the nature of love that could once be all-consuming, yet become dead and brittle like tinder, she would defend her marriage, at least to herself, believing that marriages assumed many forms, one of which was a concern, if not a love, for the partner, and a united front to meet the practicalities of a shared life.

Of course the disappearance of her love had affected their sex life. She found it hard to pretend that desire for him consumed her, but didn't deny him, lying still as he whispered endearments, as he mounted and grappled, stilled abruptly and rolled away. She would turn wordlessly towards the window, to the night sky pierced by stars and the fretting gum leaves imaging the ceiling. It was a necessary part of marriage, even of the idea of marriage that she defended. She knew that Brian had noticed the difference, but hoped that he would view it as a quirk of time, or one of the mysteries that afflict women.

'Yes, I do,' she answered Jim's question, the enquiry of all jealous lovers. 'It's important, a necessary physical part of a relationship, an important routine like putting the cat out at night. Don't worry. It's hardly the same with you.' She later felt guilty about the flippancy and disloyalty of this remark. It was important to her, a bonding and necessary part of a social contract. Besides, it was important in the current situation to maintain an agreeable relationship with her husband.

The sex with Jim was different. She knew there were critics who view affairs as the need for people to rediscover what they'd lost or never found, or as an analgesic, deadening sense of hope unsatisfied and lonely wilting marriages, a fury pounded frenziedly with wordless lust and little care against unfulfilled lives. It was different with Jim because she really loved him.

Their first time was at Jim's place. She'd gone there after the night of her book group with the excuse that they both laughed about later as lame, of returning the book the women had discussed earlier that night. He spared her the embarrassment of asking why she didn't wait, and the brewing desire – fed by yearning looks, connecting talk, innuendo, and not so accidental touch – resulted in the inevitable.

She had been unnerved when Brian surprised them on the balcony, and had been prepared for an ugly scene. But it didn't happen, and convinced that he hadn't seen, she was in no way contrite, and devised more elaborate plans to rendezvous. Their meetings were mostly at night, sometimes mid-morning, and when Jim's flat partner was home, they'd sometimes meet in the bush behind the church, a desperate choice for Jane because it made her feel dirty and somehow sacrilegious. Yet despite their creativity and best laid plans, the tug of desire between them couldn't be hidden from others, and she was aware that people had begun to talk.

An impasse had been reached: either break with Brian, and suffer the scandal of a small town broken marriage for which she would be vilified as the villain and possibly cast out with little to support herself; or end things with Jim, and suffer the pain of separation and a lifetime of wondering what might have been.

*

When he'd told her they needed to talk, she knew the time of reckoning had come. She felt a little irritated that he had asked for a meeting, when over breakfast would have sufficed, but perhaps he thought it needed a more formal occasion to carry the weight of revelation.

She looked up as he finished pacing. A numbing calm settled like an eiderdown. No, she would not dissemble. She would be quiet and reasoned, and she would try to avoid making him complicit in her behaviour, resist the temptation of providing him with a litany of his own shortcomings.

The only dilemma she had not yet resolved was whether to tell him of her love for Jim, or be dismissive, and relegate it to the status of a shabby affair. There was a faint hope that the latter could be forgiven if not forgotten in time. The implications of the former were more irrevocable.

She didn't want him to be hurt, and didn't want to be the cause of his pain. Watching him standing there awkwardly, his lips pursed in that familiar way, ready to speak, she felt some sympathy, though there was little tender feeling. It was more the sympathy you feel when anyone suffers gratuitous pain. The guilt she experienced was eased by her all-consuming love for Jim.

Watching her sitting there seemingly composed, he knew that she understood what was to come. She looked so attractive, and still aware of his love, he too wished he might have arranged things less formally. But how? A 'By the way, I've reason to believe…' between the porridge and the toast?

She was wearing the white blouse with the puffed sleeves that he liked so much, and with her hair swept back and gathered behind, she looked elegant. For a moment, he wanted to go to her and hold her, reassure her, and somehow reclaim their lost love. But from the tenderness sprang those images that tormented him, and he felt a growing hostility towards her infidelity, fed by resentment for his loss of power to control the situation.

He'd rehearsed his words, even written them down, and changed them, either softening or hardening them according to the flux of his feelings. It was a preamble he thought to be reasonable, and one that urged calmness, caring and mutual respect. But as he began, and saw her eyes watching with intent and perhaps entreaty, he simply asked the question outright.

For two or three seconds there was a heavy silence as she readied herself to answer. Even the expected can be shocking when finally acknowledged. But having asked the question, he instantly despaired, and wished he hadn't. He realised now that he didn't want to know the truth, saw the implications of knowing to be fraught with risks that threatened his dreams. He knew that realities are built with words that cause a feeling or a thought to grow, and he was fearful that the words they spoke now might create deeper truths.

And so he turned abruptly, excused himself, avoided her puzzled eyes, and hurried from the room, convinced that certainties would make him mad.

Teacher

She took them outside. Gathered them beneath the single playground tree, a jacaranda that lifted the cement path it carpeted in fibrous lilac. The children copied her, doing their stretches, star jumps and running on the spot, feeling the fibrous jacaranda bells crunch beneath their feet to wither instantly in a damp mess and lose their colour in the summer sun. She called out encouragement, and they tried to please, their faces pink, damp and intent, imitating her enthusiasm.

'Wait there,' she called, and she hurried into the classroom, pushed a tape into the old cassette player on the teacher's desk, turned up the volume and hurried back out. 'Follow me,' she called, and the children formed a conga line, each one placing hands around the waist of the child in front. They'd done it before. Part of some schooldays they really enjoyed.

She moved forward and, to the rhythm of the music, kicked one leg to the side, took a few steps, then kicked the other. The children imitated, snaking forwards, turning corners. She started to move in ways that made the children laugh. Little scurrying movements. Jumping on the spot. Throwing one hand out and calling '*olé*'. The children responded with even louder '*olés*'. As the music quickened, the dance became even more frantic and more ridiculous until the tail of the line collapsed, and the last half dozen children fell to the ground, laughing hysterically.

She smiled as she watched them, several climbing from the ground, still giggling, some flushed and breathing heavily, others watching her, waiting to demonstrate obedience in order to find the favour they craved. Excited faces. Malleable wills. Innocence.

'Back row to the bubblers first,' she called cheerily.

No one protested, and as they finished drinking, the children filed up the two worn stone steps and into the wooden classroom.

For a few seconds, she looked across the sparse, straw-coloured flat land to the shimmering haze that melted the horizon. She seemed momentarily lost in thought, but turned abruptly and followed them. 'Aiden's first for news.'

Aiden carefully pulled an old rusted cow bell from a plastic bag. 'My dad found this in the bottom paddock,' he beamed, full of importance. 'He says it's very old.'

'What a wonderful find,' she enthused, 'like a buried treasure. Let's see what sound it makes, though not too loud.'

But abetted by the obvious expectations of the other children, and Aiden's own enthusiasm, it was loud.

'I don't think a poor old cow would make it ring that loud.' She pulled a comical face. 'Do you think a cow could make its head go up and down as fast as Aiden's hand?'

The children laughed. And so did Aiden.

Several hours later, they boarded the old green and yellow school bus that rattled its way through the town, and along dirt roads to the fringes of the town, where some of the children helped with the farm work before dinner.

*

The young couple at Beecham's Boarding House, realising that she was eating her dinner alone, spoke to her from an adjoining table. There were no other guests. The boarding house was a ramshackle two-storey wooden place with a dining room and Mrs Beecham's residence on the ground floor, and six identical bedrooms above. A To Let sign hung sideways on a rusty nail by the front door, giving cock-eyed permission to would-be tenants. The house was in the main street, and the row of bedroom balconies, enclosing those who ventured onto them behind elaborately patterned wrought-iron balustrades, afforded a view across the lemony grass flats, scorched by February sun and drying winds.

'Until I find something else,' she answered them. 'I'm trying. I've let a lot of people know I'm looking.'

'We're only here for the night,' the young man told her. 'On the way to show her off to my folks,' and he squeezed the shoulder of the young woman, who smiled back enticingly.

'Do you think I'll pass muster?' the young woman quipped, searching for compliments and assuming a histrionic pose.

'Of course you will. You'll knock them dead. It was meant to be, you and me. They'll all see that. Fate. That's what it was,' and he turned to the teacher as she was making slow progress with the sausages and vegetables. 'Do you believe in fate?'

'I'm not sure,' she answered, finishing a mouthful. She thought some more. 'I suppose some things are meant to be, and there are some things we can't control, but I like to think, yes, I like to think that there are some things we can decide…or at least have a choice in deciding.'

'Yes, I like that.' The young man was directing the talk. 'I mean they don't have to be opposites, do they? When I first saw this beautiful woman at the country fair, I knew she was the one, and I decided… she was wearing jodhpurs and a tight-fitting checked blouse. Wow.' He paused to take her hand. A public confession demanded such theatre. 'I marched right up to her and asked her out.'

'And I was there with someone else,' the young woman laughed, enjoying the attention.

'He never had a chance. Poor bugger. *Carpe diem*. That's my motto. *Carpe diem*.' And he leant across the table, brandishing his fork, his mouth still part-full, and kissed the young woman on the cheek.

She stood on the balcony later that night, holding the flaking railing and looking across the hills, bathed in blackness. Even the street was black. All lights out, and the only sound a faint music from a distant jukebox or someone's radio dislocating the silence. There was a soft wind, warm and gritty. She couldn't see much. There was no moon, and land and sky were as one in the darkness. No definition. A little like life, she mused. No clear boundaries. Not the darkness. No, she wasn't like that. Not depressed. Not one of those people who think the world's a hostile place, see bad in everything.

She went inside. Perhaps tomorrow there'll be some news about somewhere to stay more permanently. A farmstead with a family she can be part of, a widow living alone and glad of the company.

She heard a bed begin to bark on the floor next door, the bedhead knocking against the wall, rhythmically yet gaining a frantic tempo. Then sudden silence. Empty silence. She pulled the heavy drapes, undressed in front of the fly-spotted mirror, and climbed into bed.

*

They weren't the normal playground noises. Not the squeals, hoots and punctuated hum of pleasure. Leaving her desk to investigate, she found two boys fighting, rolling around on the ground that had been worn of grass by the eternal pounding of children's feet, and the annoyance of dogs. Shirts out. Covered in dust and jacaranda bloom. One boy with a trickle of blood from the corner of his mouth. As she emerged suddenly into the outdoor light and heat, the boys struggled to their feet, sweating, intent, and started to throw wild punches. Very few made contact.

The other children were silent as they watched. Bewildered. Disbelieving. Morbidly fascinated. Two girls were crying.

'Stop that at once,' she called, raising her voice for the first time. But making her way towards the brawling boys to separate them, a flailing fist hit her in the chest.

The boys stopped immediately. The look of antagonism drained from their faces. Aggression became submission, and they stood with their heads down, looking blanched and chastened. The other children watched wide-eyed, all stunned by the horror of what had occurred and what it meant in the scheme of things. It was only when she had moved to sit on one of the playground benches, winded, breathing heavily, wincing, that one child approached her tentatively. Others followed, milling around her. One went for a glass of water. Others enquired, did she want a doctor? The police?

The class was quiet for the rest of the day. Even the most animated students were unusually subdued. They worked from their texts, and she watched, without her usual supervision walking up and down the rows of desks. In the middle of the afternoon, she called the two offenders to accompany her outside.

The boys were pale and frightened. She sat on the playground bench she'd occupied before, and motioned for the boys to sit either side of her. She said nothing.

After an agonising silence, one of the boys croaked, 'I'm sorry, miss,' a cue for the other to tearfully repeat the sentiment. 'It was an accident. We didn't mean for you to get hit.' Then realising that their crime went further than Miss being hurt, they kept quiet and waited for an answer.

But there wasn't one. She sat stock-still, staring across the wide-open flaxen spaces where the grass was blown one way like a Mexican wave, and then another by a capricious wind, causing it to change colour and texture as it did so.

After a minute or two – it seemed an eternity to the boys – she put an arm around the shoulders of each of them, and drew them to her. And as the minutes passed, she held them more tightly, without saying a word, and without looking at either of them. The class worked quietly inside.

*

She met him at the local club. Blue-eyed. Hair bleached blond in patches by the sun. Freckled and wearing sunburn like a farmer's boast. There was something appealing in the way he approached. Timid, even ingenuous.

'Aren't you the new teacher?' he ventured.

'Yes, still getting used to things around here. It's all a bit different. What do you do?'

'I'm a farmer,' and as an afterthought, 'dairy farmer. Long days,' he felt the need to add. 'Some people say long and smelly.'

Was it his clothes or boots she wondered, that gave off a faint, yet not unmanly whiff of hay and manure. 'What is there to do in the town?' She hoped she didn't sound critical. 'I mean for younger people.'

'Not much. A dance every month in the old town hall. Line dancing. Square dancing. Sometimes something modern.' The Country Women's Association holds fetes and poetry readings, if you like that stuff. There's a bridge club.'

He offered to buy her a drink but she didn't want it. They looked across the grasslands shimmering in the heat, and he pointed in the direction of neighbouring towns. She'd never heard of them. He named a few of the more eminent locals who entered the club – the mayor, a bearded, rotund man who was also the town undertaker; the president of the Country Women's Association, grey-haired with a blue rinse and exuding self-importance; and a brassy blonde with enormous breasts who he self-consciously described as the town bicycle.

She was hesitant in accepting a lift back to Beecham's, but it was a long walk in the heat. So she climbed into the old Ford Falcon after he'd opened the door and closed it after her. Something furry bounced from an elastic string on the rear-view mirror.

He stopped the car outside Beecham's. 'I have some strawberries from the farm in the back, some beer and a bottle of white wine that's chilled in the esky. If you like…'

She froze. Who did he think she was? Did he really think she was like that, that easy, like the brassy blonde in the club, perhaps a new and more refined town bicycle? Frantic, she whispered a peremptory 'No', opened the door, and ran into the boarding house, stopping only to pick up a shoe that came off in her flight, ran up the stairs into her room, closed the door and threw herself onto the bed.

She lay perfectly still, expecting any moment to hear a knock or banging on the door. The drapes were open so she dared not reveal herself in the light of the window. She strained to hear, but there was silence. Perhaps he was listening outside, wondering whether to try the door. He might be sweet-talking Mrs Beecham to gain himself unlimited access. Then the faint sound of an engine coming to life, and she saw the Falcon slowly pull away.

*

The children worked quietly. There'd been no conga line dance this morning, and they assumed that Miss was still upset from what had happened with the fight on Friday. She hadn't been her usual sunny self. While only two boys were at fault, Miss had said a few days before that the whole class had to accept responsibility for the behaviour of all of them. She called it a collective responsibility. 'Can anyone spell "collective"? Let's sound it out together.'

It was even hotter than usual. The distant yellows and oranges in the haze made the grass appear to be on fire. Tangerine against a ming-blue sky. A brisk wind blew heat across the room.

'Tomorrow, but only if it's cooler, we'll do the conga line dance. I want you all to think of some different steps, funny steps if you like, but they have to fit the music.'

The children were delighted, and relieved that Miss was back to how she used to be. But it didn't escape the more perceptive that her eyes were a little pink and swollen.

Brother

The morning my brother died I was mowing the lawn. It was early winter and the grass greened free from the silver whiskers of frost. The news came by phone, brutal, fired at point-blank range. His wife had been driving the car that ran off the road near Wollombi, threaded its way through some trees and came to rest upside down in a narrow river that had been dry only six weeks before. My brother and his only child were drowned. His wife floated free. A man following in a car behind had dived repeatedly but to no avail. The water was dark and freezing.

My first response was incredulity. Emotion lags behind a sudden blow, as if the meanings need to settle. Its impact would soon follow, yet not so much as the usual expression of grief, but more as an ether, a suffering without feeling that blunted my world without my being fully aware of it. It was more a challenge to a life of certainties, and the problem of making it intelligible in a grander scheme.

My parents were on a bowls holiday in Dubbo. 'I have some terrible news,' I told my father on the phone. A pause for us both to brace. 'Richard and Sally have both been killed.'

A halt to digest, and I sensed his palpable struggle. Then haltingly, 'Well, tell me what happened, son.'

The harrowing need to recover, to critique. I explained, outlining the grocery list of detail that would escalate over the next few days and be parroted as therapy for months, the incantation of bereavement, and its not-so-subtle search for empathy, the thirst for consolation.

'So what do you think we should do?' Helplessness disguised as collaboration.

'What is it, Owen?' I could hear my mother urging in the background, her terror acute.

'Just wait a minute,' he told her, control reasserting, and he made hasty arrangements with me to meet at the hospital later that day.

Again I could hear my distraught mother.

'Can you wait a minute,' he hesitated. Relent. Control. 'I'll have to tell your mother.'

I heard the barely audible 'Richard's died and Sally too.' And I heard her grief and the consoling sounds of flocking women.

It may have been a typical coping with grief for that generation – her pain without check, his vaunted male stoicism and struggling faith in reason. I'd been drafted as confederate in the male business of making the decisions. And I was a little uneasy about it.

I remember the neatness of Cessnock Hospital as I sat in the car with my wife awaiting my parents' arrival, and the unusual awareness of the details of textured brick and lawn and would-be cheerful flowers, as if they had significance. Perhaps it was the challenge of their immutability, timelessness, or the lameness of their attempt to uplift. I felt like the covetous guardian of a tombstone. And Richard lay somewhere inside in final wooden sleep. I kept imagining how he, a devotee of style, would rate this end: the crisp and sunny blue of the day and the provincial modesty of the place. Perhaps I was searching for meanings, for symbols, or ironies. Was it presumption for the sun to thaw the winter frost now that he was gone? Should arthritic trees continue to flex and stretch in timeless unconcern?

His wife lay pale but unhurt in a hospital bed, and her family was already there, fussing. There was little more she could tell us. My father viewed Richard's body and emerged from the mortuary annex pale-faced, a hint of trembling about a clenched mouth. We shook the moist-fishness of the attendant's single hand. The absence of the other seemed somehow grotesque. I don't know why I didn't view the body. It's supposed to help loved ones accept the awful finality. I didn't need convincing. It's thought to provide the chance to say goodbye. But to who or what are such goodbyes made? I wonder now if it was a form of cowardice.

In the week and months ahead, I anticipated that pain would pall my sense, yet slowly lead me to greater understanding. At times I'd escape to the porch at dark of night and hug the cold. The sentience of the bush with its heavy scents and cricket noises would bring Richard nearer. And I'd conspire with him in wry asides.

*

I shared a bedroom with Richard in the humble two-bedroom apricot brick Eastwood home. In primary school years, after our ritual diet of fifteen-minute radio serials, we would run our own serials in bed. These were verbal improvisations and I have no recollection what they were about except that we adopted the unlikely names of 'Carrot' and 'Cauliflower'. Names emerge mysteriously from childhood cultures just as they do between lovers. Perhaps carrot and cauliflower, vegies my mother commonly served, are little different from the amorous sobriquets of 'Petal Pie' or 'Snookums'.

Before I acquired my own room at the age of fourteen, a tiny converted sun room in which I surrounded myself with books, the comfortable artefacts of all knowing, Richard and I studied together in the downstairs tool room. I had a tiny trestle table painted bright yellow, and rough wooden boxes labelled with the peeling paper stickers of 'Perry's Fruit and Veg' to store my books. The light was dim, and overhead a mesh of intersecting pipes whined with the house's plumbing. Beside my desk, a trapdoor to the black and forbidden bowels of the house did little to muffle the scurrying noises beyond it.

In our teenage years we competed. Two years older, Richard had the edge, but the advantage diminished with my growing size and strength. We would wrestle on the front lawn, reddened by the nettle of buffalo grass. Success in these 'never-say-die' contests carried the dreams of incipient manhood. We played competition tennis together, though not always amicably. I was more intense than him, though nonchalance is often a disguise, just as prudery is a mask for the libertine. One day, irked by something I said, he deliberately threw a game, quickly serving four double faults. I hated him for that.

Richard was gifted. He did particularly well at school. That, and my more demonstrable social aplomb led to a typecasting by my parents. Richard was the clever one. I was the social one. The different perception was even expressed in the pullovers my mother lovingly knitted: blue or green for Richard, and red or yellow for me.

Beyond school, we both went to university, though took separate social paths. My milieu was a church group conferring a tacit if ill-defined morality. It was didactic but too uncertain of itself to be sanctimonious. Richard's social group was an odd assortment. Apart from the Young Liberals, some were friends who drifted in and out of unskilled employment.

Family saw Richard as reserved and unemotional. His photographs were always unsmiling. They hovered between haughtiness and a studied indifference. Of course such outward appearances are often masks worn for so long that they become realities. And so I thought it was for Richard. I always remember him leaving the house for his first driver's licence test, whistling with exaggerated nonchalance. I knew he was terrified.

Yet how much of what we present to the world is the true essence of our being? How much of what we see in anyone is not refracted by the lens of our own experience? Is indifference, or feigned indifference, really a fear to engage in the risky business of emotion? Are sensitivity, diplomacy, and even civilisation the adulterators of other realities?

*

Richard married a few years before I did, and became ensconced as a solicitor in a small law firm. He assumed all the trappings of the nouveau riche, legacy not so much of a well paid job, but of a very substantial profit from Tasminex shares. He built a modern-style house with two storeys and a cathedral ceiling in St Ives, became part owner of a number of racehorses, and for a number of years drove a silver Maserati. His first visit in the new car to the humble family home seemed like the meeting of two cultures. We watched in awe and took turns at sitting in each of the two bucket seats while Richard expended more than the usual quota of disguised delight.

But his marriage remained childless, even after I became a father. One pervasive image I have is of my son Scott, a curly blond with blue eyes, and barely two years old, tottering towards Richard, arms outstretched, with all the faith and candour of a child. It's hard to say whether it was the infertility of his marriage, or the challenge of emotion that made Richard baulk. His wife showed no interest in either of my children, and while I could appreciate their own disappointment, it seemed mean-spirited. Time, though, has its way of etiolating perceptions like these.

Some nine years after application, Sally was adopted, and the thaw in Richard became apparent. I saw a tenderness and paternalism I'd never seen before. He held Sally with overt pride, and the warmth spilled over into his relationship with me. It was still familiar rather than close, but I sensed for the first time that, as a brother, I was valued at least covertly.

I felt this same consanguinity when I observed the likeness between Richard and my now seven-year-old Scott. At particular angles, there was a strong resemblance, and similar mannerisms. The change in Richard was apparent one day when he and his wife visited our Dural house to play tennis, and were greeted by Scott at the letter box. Richard allowed Scott to sit between his legs and gave him the impression of steering the car down the pebble drive. Perhaps he sensed the link as well.

I don't know whether Richard was becoming his true self, discarding the brittle shell that had protected his fragility, or whether this was some deeper transformation. I've often thought of Nietzsche's claim that we become who we are. If this is so, who are we before we 'become'? Aren't we just continually evolving, changing with circumstance and experience, only entitled to claim 'arriving' at the time of death? Perhaps not even then.

Like many two-year-olds, Sally was very plump. I felt little affinity for the large and rubbery pink blob with a bloated face, and probably blamed her condition on the indulgence of parents. It was a different little girl, though, a year later on Mother's Day 1983, taking my hand at the Kuring-gai Wildlife Gardens. I was the chosen walking companion of a slim, fair-haired girl in a party frock, socks and sandals. I discovered her for the first time, like Richard had with a more expansive heart a couple of years earlier. She held my hand tightly and we chatted and laughed like conspirators. I never saw her again.

*

It's Father's Day 2000, and we visit my father in the dementia wing of the nursing home. Scott and my daughter Lara are there for me. My mother and I are there for my father. It is hot and blue outside, and sulphur-crested cockatoos swoop between the towering gums. My father raises an arm of crepe in silent salute. I'm still moved by the irony that he might have an empathy with these free spirits.

We exchange gifts: books for me, consumables for him. He has long since lost the ability to appraise the value of things. There is no reaction, though he seems to nod when we joke about raiding his chocolates. The talk is perfunctory and forced, though we try to include him.

I turn to Scott. 'Richard…' I begin and hesitate.

Scott smiles. No one else reacts. I surprise myself after all these years. After the anaesthetic of suffering without feeling, my healing skin of glossy pink has become a calloused hide. Children have been reared, a marriage has failed, I have a new partner, and my father has escaped to a world that is surely safe from thoughts of his long-dead elder son. And my mother survives, tough and resilient. I realise that the time is coming when I will be the only one left from that modest brick house in Eastwood.

I think of the pewter-framed photograph of my brother that stands gathering dust on my mother's dresser. It's the mature if still enigmatic Richard, even sporting a beard, his usual indifference warmed by just a hint of complacent smile. It has probably already become the stuff of party games on family likenesses. And I ask myself if anyone in private moments of quiet reflection wonders whether he once felt a searing love or a rarefied emotion, whether he railed against injustice or retreated like a child.

Will anyone, after the fun of squawker blow-outs, between the whoops of party game laughter, enquire, perhaps a little impatiently, 'Yes, I know he's related, I know the stories about him, but what was he really like?'

'Richard,' I begin again. Was it just the mottled shadow from the swaying gums, or did my father smile?

Accident

He still recalls the egg of flesh, the oval convexity of thigh in the torn gape of her stocking, its plumped whiteness, even in the revolving rufus lights from the police car and ambulance that muddied the dusk and signed the accident with a tell-tale shade of blood.

It was the corner of Abercrombie and George. She was hit while crossing at the lights, thrown onto the car's bonnet, and had slid off into the gutter where she lay motionless with her head against the kerb, and one leg bent beneath her. The elderly woman driver sat still in her car in obvious shock, and an impatient driver blew his horn behind her, not having seen the reason for her stopping.

It could easily have been me, he thought, for he had hesitated a moment before crossing to retrieve some coins that had fallen from a hole in his pocket, and had seen the incident unfold.

He hurried across to where she lay, wishing that he'd completed the first-aid course his work had sponsored earlier that year. Some ghouls had already gathered, not bothering to help, and were watching silently, their faces flared in the spasmodic light.

The woman appeared to be in her forties, though it was difficult to read her features, for her face had reassembled to cope with what she was suffering. Her eyes were darting about, trying to assess the implications of what had happened. He could smell her fear.

Her arm was raised like Rodin's supplicating hand, from which there was a small trickle of blood like a macabre theatrical plot. He placed his briefcase of soft leather beneath her head on the kerb to afford some relief, self-consciously pulled down her dress that had twisted around her waist, and held the raised hand. Her frantic eyes settled on his, and focused, reading her pain in his face.

'Is there anything I can do to make you more comfortable?' he asked.

She didn't answer, but after a brief pause in a dove-like whisper, she entreated, 'Don't ever leave me. Promise me,' searching his eyes.

And what surprises him even now, was his own requited response. 'I'll never leave you,' trumping every statement of feeling he'd ever made, and he felt a slight squeeze of his hand as her eyes misted.

The cavalry arrived, a fanfare of light and sound, and he was ushered away by the paramedics. 'Are you her husband?' one of them asked him as she was stretchered into an ambulance.

A policeman was flagging motorists into a single inquisitive lane. Stuart still recalls a hole in the sole of her shoe, the size of a ten-cent coin as the trolley slid away.

Later that night he kept replaying her words over and over. It wasn't 'don't leave me', or even 'promise you won't leave me'. It was the emphasis given to the stand alone 'promise', and the inclusion of the eternal 'ever'. He wanted to see her. Of course he had to see that she was all right. But he needed to validate the emotion they'd shared, to live the power of feeling that had flared so dramatically. It shouldn't be too difficult to obtain her name and that of the hospital.

Lying restlessly in bed that night, he tried to draw a picture of her life from the groceries strewn across the road from the impact, the sad accessories of simple living, the bircher muesli and frozen berries, the pair of tights and the Elseve balsam.

*

'I saw Santa's boot, Dad,' the six-year-old Stuart McGlynn told his father.

'Did you really? I never did when I was growing up.' His father was enthusiastic in sustaining Stuart's elation. 'Sylvie, Stuart saw Santa's boot,' he said aloud to his grinning wife.

This was to be the first of many fancies typical of the growing child. It soon became apparent that Stuart had unusual sensitivities and a strong sense of justice. At the age of seven, having just watched a news report on another terrorist attack, he asked his father whether the world would be a better place if everyone 'was kind to each other'.

'Well yes, it would,' his father replied, putting down the evening paper and sensing one of those formative connections between father and son.

'Then why doesn't the government make everyone be kind?' Stuart persisted.

'A lot of people find it hard to be kind all the time,' and his father tried to explain, talking of the different and sometimes clashing values that people hold, and using Stuart's very occasional naughty lapses as an example of the law's limitations.

Stuart would bring home stray cats and dogs and hide them in the garden shed, sneaking out at night to bring them some of the dinner that he'd stuffed into his pockets. He was caught out one night when one of the scruffy stray dogs scratched on the kitchen door in the early hours of the morning and woke his parents. After constant and tearful pleading, he was allowed to keep the dog that they all agreed should be called Scruffy. He cried inconsolably when a neighbour, Mr Reid, disposed of a litter of newly born cats by flushing them down the toilet.

Once in secondary school, Stuart acquired an interest in girls, and the hormonal changes were apparent in his physique. The only agency of his sex education was a book *Attaining Manhood*, offered uneasily by his father before his quick retreat and unfinished, out the door, 'If there's anything…' to leave him studying the ink diagrams of his reproductive bits, that caused him some anxiety about how his wriggly things assaulted eggs, reminding him of the old chook house beneath the mulberry tree.

For most of his classmates, sex was something crude inflicted upon hapless girls and celebrated with boasts and smuttiness, and talk of hyperbolic body parts. While Stuart experienced the same febrile torments of desire, he couldn't share their crudity. When, in a rare moment of disclosure, he confided his concern to one of his like-minded mates, he was not unkindly dubbed a romantic.

Stuart found two definitions of the word when he googled it: 'characterised by or suggestive of an idealised view of reality' and 'characterised by the expression of love'. This was an epiphany for Stuart. He riffled through a forgotten drawer and found an old school magazine, opening it at a poem he'd written a couple of years before, and containing the lines

> When the pink heavens glowed and you with your find
> Danced upon frothy waters chased by a nebulous sky.

He cringed when he read it. What exactly did he mean by it? Whatever did his peers and his teachers think of it? But within the obscure and flowery prose, Stuart could detect the idealised view of the world, and the evidence of love.

These expressions of the romantic were not confined to fantasy. He could never be a confederate of his classmates when they baited and teased Leonie Watkiss, the French teacher, making her cry. Where was the satisfaction in that? He couldn't abide bullying or inflicting gratuitous hurt.

In his time at school, he developed a growing interest in the Arthurian legend. He particularly liked the history of Lancelot, the greatest knight of them all, and his lover Guinevere, not so much for Lancelot's skill as a swordsman, but for the more courtly conventions, the stylised behaviours, and the respect and reverence for women.

When he left school to work with a small printing company, Stuart met Chantelle Fayne, his first love. It was to prove a love from afar because Chantelle was always surrounded by other men in the firm. He was grateful that she was pleasant to him, saying 'Hello' and enquiring after him, as he admired her violet eyes that seemed to dance in the light and twinkle with an irony that matched her melody of laugh.

Stuart was enraptured by her feminine ways, her warming blush of modesty and a natural reserve. His imagined fictions saw the heat of her arm resting on his own, smelled the scent of jasmine in her hair, and invented deep and knowing looks swapped between them, with words that were more intimate than touch. And there were of course more earthy imaginings.

His infatuation lasted for a year until the company's Christmas party, where he saw Chantelle sitting with her dress hitched up almost to her thighs, baring the full length of her shapely legs, finger-tweaking a cigarette in theatrical pose to orchestrate affected talk, and taking unconcealed delight as men competed to fill her glass, seduced by a flamboyant laugh.

Stuart watched, feeling his fantasies drain, her sweetness disappear, her face reassemble, and her voice's music become discordant. He was left with the pain of his stricken fantasies in a lonely illusory world, realising that the roads towards the emerald city are often paved by broken stone.

Jean was his first real love, a girl he'd known at school, a girl with strong intellectual interests and little attraction to the physical. She admired his idealism, believing it had its origins in a thoughtful consideration of what makes the world go round.

At first, Jean and Stuart chatted for hours, revelling in sharing insights and surprised to find that what they had previously regarded as unique wasn't so unique after all. They believed themselves to be soulmates. But as the romance faded, and as the selective nature of their talk was exhausted, there were longer periods of uneasy silence that Jean tried to fill in the only way she knew how, to address an issue or analyse feeling, thought or motive.

'Why do we have to intellectualise everything?' he asked her. 'Why do we have to tease apart every emotion, explain our feeling? Perhaps to reason it is to destroy it.' He despaired at the absence of laughter. There was never any sense of the ridiculous. Life was something to be mangled of its juice, to be wrung out to dry.

Unseen, he watched her the following week waiting at the bus stop, looking frail and spiritless, wearing a tight dress that flattened and straightened her figure, making her look like a primary school boy, biting her lip with the constant anxiety she suffered. She might need protection, he thought, but Stuart knew then that he was not the one to provide it. She was no longer appealing, and even the self-conscious and wooden sex had lost its allure. They separated without a whimper.

Now forty-two, Stuart has never married. He lives alone, and has been promoted to assistant manager in a rival printing company. He visits his ageing and ailing parents each weekend to do the chores they can no longer manage, plays bridge once a week, and is writing a romantic novel.

*

He felt buoyant as he entered the hospital, strode past the leather lounges in the foyer to the reception desk, and asked for the room number. He'd overdressed at first, before he decided on informality. 'Smart casual', work invitations used to read, and so he chose the tan trousers and black pullover. He'd stood for an eternity in front of the mirror, trimming eyebrows and removing ear and nose hair.

Entering the florist's in the foyer, he selected a bunch of red roses, dismissed the message they carried as presumptuous for this early in a relationship, and exchanged them for a mix of yellow, orange and red gerberas.

He was mindful of the mythology of attraction at times like this, that the possibility of imminent death generated the tug of sex, some primal urge, or regenerative instinct. How many times had he heard that response, usually saucy yet sometimes quite serious, to the question of what you would do if you knew the world would end in an hour? The sexual urge for him was not predominant. It was the power of his feeling.

Stuart would be seeing her soon. He'd been thinking of little else, and had allowed three days to ensure that she had recovered and felt a little more robust. He had checked on her progress by phone, but had not left his name. Her words had assumed an indelible magic, 'Don't ever leave me. Promise me,' and there was the hint of her hand squeezing his as she said them.

And what was even more remarkable was the impact for him of his own words, 'I'll never leave you.' From the moment he said them, he was in awe that so much in his life had changed, that nothing could take away that acknowledgement, the rendered words that freed his guarded heart.

And surely it was the same for her. He imagined what she might feel when she woke up in the hospital, having lapsed into unconsciousness on the road side, looking up into a stranger's caring face that held her pain.

'Ever,' she'd whispered. It was their private commitment. Twice now he'd pranced around his bedroom like a small, excited child, or a man possessed, and chanting 'ever ever ever ever ever'.

He took the lift, still buoyant, mindful of the symbolism of ascension, and was directed to her room, pausing outside to ready himself after the never-ending days and wakeful nights.

Several people were bunkered around the bed, concealing his view. Two were older, probably her mother and father, one was a younger girl, and there was a man her same age who had his hand resting affectionately on her shoulder. They all turned when he entered and stopped talking. Taken by surprise, he realised how foolish he'd been, not having reckoned on her having company. Why did he assume there'd be no other significant people in her life. Quickly recovering, he moved to the bedside, feeling gauche as he offered the flowers with a lame 'Remember me?'

'Oh yes,' she replied after a few seconds, as if the realisation were slow to dawn. 'You're the man…' She left the sentence unfinished, and what must have been a few seconds seemed like hours, as the family members watched with interest, perhaps suspicion, and shifted their feet.

A nurse checked the clipboard at the base of the bed and retreated.

'Just wanted to see how you are,' Stuart said rather too loudly.

There was another long pause.

'I should thank you,' she said. 'What you did was kind,' and there was a mixed chorus of disinterested thanks from all those around the bed, followed by another uneasy silence, a signal for him to retire so that they could resume family business.

Escaping to the door, and conscious of being watched, his tread seems unnaturally loud on polished linoleum. Once outside, he hears the muted talk resume inside the room. Someone laughs. He walks slowly, unseeing, along the corridor, and past the nurses' station, where antiseptic bites and loiters. Nurses hurry past him zealously as if he isn't there. He smiles ruefully. It's just one more time that passion charged, lost heart and fled.

Signature

His errant fancy half-expected Dickens, wooden benches in an airless room abutting squalid alleyways, an oil lamp coughing feeble light, and he, an evil-smelling and opportunistic Fagin with a limp or tic. But his wife's lawyer is not a 'he', and she is no smiling assassin, but more like someone's neighbour tending roses on a Sunday afternoon. She seems a pleasant enough woman, stylish in her pinstripe suit.

He isn't used to the city, and while he's drawn to its colour and motion, its feast of sight and sound, its pungent smells, he finds it a little forbidding, too teeming with life. As the lift climbs noiselessly to the eighth floor, he wonders what he has let himself in for, but there is no turning back now. The greeting is formal and polite, befitting a business transaction, and in a small, bare office with décor of grey and salmon pink, he's ushered to a leather chair behind a mahogany desk.

*

He could still see the accusation in his wife's eyes as she leafed through her score of the previous night's interview to find inconsistencies. She'd interrogate him for an hour, writing speedily on the back of used computer paper to record actual phrases and sentences. Conciliation was important for him, so for a few days he submitted to the inquisition about the values he held dear, his capacity to feel and respond, the way he behaved. She transcribed the dialogue, and confronted him the following nights, venomously calling him a liar, and citing what she interpreted to be inconsistencies in the transcript.

They attended counselling on a few occasions, but she called a halt when the counsellor, undertaking what they both believed to be the probably impossible task of teasing out what had gone wrong, seemed to be showing more sympathy for him than for her. He'd always seen her call for counselling as a subterfuge, a way of justifying her actions to an unforgiving world that she'd later court with tales of his duplicity. The decision had already been made. The counselling was a charade, acting out a deluded self-righteousness.

For several months, she'd moved into the guest bedroom, continued her work with a manic intensity, and treated him with a restrained politeness. From outward appearances, things continued as normal. He tended to the garden, did much of the housework, and drove his children to their sporting commitments, and she shopped and cooked. But she was increasingly late home from work, often between eight and nine at night.

She gave the final ultimatum, though he knew it had to come, that there's a point in doomed relationships when something once formidable can never be reclaimed. After having considered moving out herself, she now thought it appropriate that he go. The children were the primary consideration, and she claimed to be in a better position to care for them. He's still uncertain as to why he acquiesced. Was it the pervasive guilt we feel when something that belongs to us, something for which we are accountable, fails, or was it a belief that her claim about the children's welfare may have been true? In harsher moments of self-criticism, he wondered if he had become, or always had been, a victim.

He was the one to talk to his thirteen and fifteen-year-old children at a family meeting. It was no time for recrimination. It was rather a time to admit that Mum and Dad preferred to live apart, and to convince his son and daughter that the dislocation would not be too great, and that they were in no way to blame. A time to reassure that neither parent would withdraw their love, and would always be there for them. Both children listened quietly and retired shaken to their rooms without a word. He knew their palpable silence could not have been indifference. It seemed to speak more than a thousand words.

*

Sitting opposite him, the lawyer assumes a relaxed informality, but familiarity is out of the question. It would be normal for him to reach out to another, jest perhaps, even when he's suffering or under threat, but this is just too big. He's oppressed by a burden that weighs too much, and he feels numb, spiritless.

The papers are already on the desk and, as there is no need for the lawyer to detail the purpose of the meeting, she begins to peel the pages with her soapy fingers, briefly explaining the document. He watches with morbid fascination. Each turned page seems like an indictment, a passing of sentence. There is a suggestion of pleasures eau de toilette, and he sees the lawyer's earrings catch the sun that cuts a swathe into the room. Handing over a black biro, she points to the first pencil cross, Golgotha of a doomed relationship.

*

Leaving home, his rustic dream, he watched the few sticks of furniture he'd been allocated, hauled across the driveway stones that scrunched beneath the stolid boots of the removalists, robust men manoeuvring boxes past the beds of his lovingly tended roses (white ice, Caroline) now sadly out of bloom, and then to his new home, a top-floor unit fifteen kilometres away, interment in a laneway tagged 'industrial' and weeping for its poverty of sentiment.

For sixteen months, he'd climb the stairs that he always regarded as a symbol of loss, imagining that he was spiralling inwards, feeding his introspection, climbing the dirty mustard carpet cheerlessly lit by sixty watts. It was a bitter foil to the acres of open bushland and the luminous gum-flagged drive that was still his, at least in name, and it left him diminished. He sometimes referred to his upstairs 'garret', the conventional literary retreat of impoverished artists.

His wife came that first day, possibly as appeasement for the children, who still battled to understand. The kettle, colander and scouring pads with meagre food for one were her last goodbye. The rest was up to him. And in that stupefying day, the image that remains, perhaps because it strips living back to its bare skeletal bones, is when she meted out three knives, three forks and three spoons.

Never having lived alone, he began the routine of providing for himself, returning from the shops that were thankfully nearby, to cook his basic meals, often taken from a cardboard box. He felt dispossessed, struck even from the message bank of children and his dog that welcomed callers to his home.

Sometimes he'd walk around the mall simply to be among people, feeling an overwhelming, almost tearful tenderness for the frazzled mother with a bawling child, or the old man at the checkout counting copper with his rheumatoid fingers from an ancient beaded purse. His missing of his children was almost beyond bearing, and he began to rail against the injustice, feeling like Lear, that he was more sinned against than sinning. Apart from the pain, there was the opiate of nothingness, all his actions dulled to joyless rituals like the bygone party's sad balloon that's lost its ripening breath and crumples limp on a stick.

Feeling like an émigré in culture shock, bloodied from his wounds, he tried to establish new routines. He increased his exercise regime to a punishing level. He visited his ageing parents on the central coast each weekend, throwing himself into demanding physical work. His daughter came sometimes, and there was comfort in their sharing the only spare bedroom, but he had to collect and return her. His wife would not assist.

In these first weeks away, the relentless incantation of separation or divorce began, with all its pained self-justifications and search for accord. He was mindful of not boring his friends with detail that they didn't really want to know, and of not dwelling on his own innocence or nobility, but sometimes the temptation was too great.

In those first months, his wife demonised him. In making him the villain, she was implicitly making herself the heroine. Believing her son had been exposed to his negative influence, she insisted that he undertake pencil and paper exercises that she devised and that were designed to set him on the right path, exercises like nominating three things he could do each day to affirm rather than find fault with his sister. She arranged for him to be taken out by her best friend's husband, believing him to be a more desirable influence. His son did not enjoy the experience, and his gratified father knew that their confederacy had survived.

*

A gentle word reminds, and as he takes the pen, the pointing finger with its blood-red nail relaxes on the page.

'No need to hurry,' she says, and the softness of her voice is complemented by a caressing manner. 'There are a few places you have to sign.'

She understands, he realises, grateful for the little warmth and humanity that she's introduced into the contract, and that she feels is professionally appropriate. Now that he's seen the spot on the page, she withdraws her finger, but remains sitting opposite, a model of decorum.

Signing at the first pencil cross, he wonders what the signature reveals of him. It's sober, compact and legible, rather than flamboyant with loops and flourishes. He's unusually sensitive to how he's perceived, and how he now perceives himself.

'Would you like a glass of water?' she asks. Yes, she understands, this heroine of the Sunday rose, and dealer in momentous wretchedness.

*

A few months pass. It's Christmas Day, and the chimera of purpose coaxes him beyond the self-deluding comforts of a bed to seek a silent fellowship yet again among the faceless strangers at the mall. Perhaps a cheery blessing, several words of festive cheer, or the sight of wide-eyed children towed by doting mums, but all is ghostly quiet.

It's still early and rags of graphite cloud deprive the day of sunlight's lustre. The street lights blaze with golden sutures in the gloom. He threads his way through broken stone and shards of glass on a demolished corner block, and newsprint blows around his feet, the crumpled news of lost-forever yesterdays. He thinks of Eliot's ancient women gathering fuel from vacant lots. There'll be many times like this now, he tells himself, waking alone on significant days.

He still feels anger towards her when he thinks of her proposed settlement. It is of course weighted heavily in her favour because the children's welfare must be uppermost. Any negotiation between them reaches that end. It is a stick she uses to beat him with. Yet with the anger he directs at her disguised self-interest, indifference is growing like a cataract across an eye.

He'd recently entered the house to fetch his daughter for the weekend, and caught his wife hurrying naked from the shower. He was surprised and saddened by his reaction. It was so unerotic, the slight distaste of stumbling into the fleshy crudities of a public change room. From that time, he was forbidden entry to the house and had to knock and wait for his daughter or son to emerge.

Some idealistic part of him resented such shifts in human emotion, from love to pain to nothingness. Such a metamorphosis seemed so capricious, robbing love of the status that it should enjoy, *omnia vincit amor*. And yet it was necessary for renewal, for his moving on and possibly finding someone else, though he believed he never would. God forbid that he should continue to love her in the way he once had.

He dreamt once of meeting her in a park some years into the future, the binding words in bedroom dark long-forgotten, their initial interest in each other loitering and dying; he saddened by her thickening with age, and she pensive as she appraises him, the old man young or the young man old.

He knows that we constantly reconstruct our realities, and so it has been for him as he keeps revisiting what has happened, finding new truths and dismissing what he now considers might be problematic, and each time applying a different lens to interpret. But it is still raw. It will be some time yet, if ever, that he won't see himself as a victim of a grave injustice.

*

Descending in the lift and emerging from the granite and the glass that muscles out the warm benignity of sky, reality still lags. He muses at the simplicity of how a signature can lay bare a life. A second's all it takes. He's been living the implications of the decision that was made for him for quite some time. Now there is a crushing finality.

Her lawyer had thanked him and shook his hand. Perhaps there was a little sympathy there, a feeling that her advocacy had cost him dearly, or it may simply have been a resigned sadness at people's capacity to hurt each other.

He's dazzled by the light as he leaves the building. The peak-hour crowd is jostling its way home. A few passers-by seem irritated that he remains stationary on the footpath, blocking their way.

'Has justice rendered me my due?' he asks himself. 'Or have I just succumbed, a victim of my own self-belief, or of life's caprice?'

The carbon-scented air is heavy with noiseless dreams.

Imagination

Why is it that a particular poem or a paragraph in a novel, a certain painting or image, or a specific piece of music, transmits a magic power enough to touch the soul, to open feeling's sluice gates for emotion's flood?

We often find ourselves disappointed when the impact we feel is not felt by others. Is it something that we've seen, heard or experienced before, perhaps some exhilarating episode in our infant years, long forgotten in the welter of life's experiences that is suddenly reawakened, struck like a match in the dark? Some explain it by claiming that it is transmitted to them through the genes, and search the sepia photographs of their stiffly frocked forebears as if they might provide a clue.

Another view is that we live multiple lives, and certain likes and dislikes, or even particular talents or idiosyncrasies, are residue from previous incarnations. We've all heard people characterise others with the strange notion that they are 'old souls', as if they possess some special inherent insight or wisdom, a view that seems to be an implicit criticism of those of us who, for whatever reason, are dubbed 'young souls'. And yet what can explain the extraordinary affinity we sometimes feel for a particular room in a house we've only just visited, or for an unknown village in another country we see on television, experiences that compel us to react with 'I feel at home here. I've been there before.'

*

I know her well, the girl who's painted on my Norman Rockwell plate, a plate on a vertical stand given pride of place on a bookshelf opposite my study desk. I even wonder if we were once close. The girl doesn't have a name, but the limited edition plate, with its identifying number and stamp, and its certificate of authenticity, bears the caption *A Young Girl's Dream*, and was painted by Rockwell in 1930. Her picture fills the twenty-one-centimetre-diameter plate.

It's appropriate that the painter's son has written on the back of the plate that the picture portrays, 'the hope and courage that are an essential part of the American dream', because the girl is supposedly waiting for a bus or train to take her to a life of promise. She is sitting on an old wooden bench in a drab and discoloured waiting room floored with wooden planks. She has two worn suitcases, one at her feet, and the other on the bench beside her. She is nursing a small red purse. Delicate and feminine, she's dressed in a modest, fitting, apple-green dress that's flounced below her pressed together knees. She is wearing a gold jacket and a white ermine scarf. The rest could well be cliché. She is slim and attractive, with shy blue eyes, blush-coloured cheeks, a softened redness in her lips unshaped by damask line, full-bodied golden ringlets of hair resting on her shoulders, and a distant look averted from the gaze of fantasists like me.

I'm well aware that the reason I find her so beguiling says more about me than her. Others would not share my perception. They might well see her as just another young woman pursuing fame or fulfilment. I know too that imagination is thought by some to be the consolation for disappointments in a person's life, but I don't believe that to be true in my case.

*

I was standing in a wide, cobbled street enclosed by period buildings that were not sufficiently tall to muscle out the pale blue sky. It must have been morning in a city business district as people thronged the streets, going about their affairs, the men in three piece suits or plus fours with butterfly-collared shirts and black ties, and the women in V-necked cardigans, simple blouses and wrap skirts. Some wore long dresses.

'Careful!' The shout came simultaneously with a screeching horn, and arms reached out to pull me to the curb as a cherry-red 1930s Buick with its tilted grill and separate drum-formed headlights careered around the corner. The sunshades on the windscreen blocked my view of the driver, and its footboard brushed my trousered leg but did no harm.

'Maniac,' the helping man muttered.

'Are you all right, sir?' a middle-aged woman in a long free-flowing pleated dress, asked with obvious concern, and began to brush the padded shoulder of my suit with a delicate hand, though I couldn't imagine why it needed brushing. 'You have to be careful in the big city,' and she smiled to put me at my ease. 'I hope it didn't make a mess of your nice suit, sir.'

I thanked her, and inspected my clothes. The straight, wide-leg trousers were still neatly pressed, and the coat, slightly nipped at the waist and with full sleeves, had not been disturbed. Even my striped necktie was firmly in place. The attentive woman handed me my fedora hat that she had rescued from the gutter, and that half a minute ago had been tipped over one eye at a rakish angle.

Recovered, I looked around the buildings. Most didn't have signs, except for the several tea rooms that seemed to have animal names. There was The Green Frog a few doors down and, behind where I had been rescued, The Brown Owl, enticing with cream teas (scones, jam and clotted cream) and high teas with a menu of savoury food.

Directly across the street, The Green Pheasant was nestled between the offices of Chevrolet and Turner's Emporium, and behind the low window that separated her from the pavement, my Rockwell plate girl sat alone with the same distant or absent-minded look, offering a profile view of her frontal picture on the plate.

Of course she wore the same apple-green dress and gold jacket, and there didn't as yet appear to be any food on the table. I watched with curiosity and pleasure, feeling the old familiarity and tenderness, tempted, yet fearing to cross the street to get closer to her, lest she see me and wonder at my interest. I wanted the long-anticipated sense of being close, but there was nothing explicitly sexual, no desire for fraught embrace, to come together as lovers. My yearning was more rarefied; dare I say, more pure.

After a couple of minutes watching, as people circled me on the pavement with increasing interest, it occurred to me that she might be waiting for someone. I admit to feeling disappointed, and decided to wait a few more minutes to see if someone arrived for her, yet my bruised feelings were tempered by a strange notion that some pleasures are best experienced from a distance, that some realities are best transcended, lest our contact might cause something precious to break. What was my motive here after all?

After what seemed a lifetime, I crossed the road obliquely, dodging a fast-approaching Austin coupé, and stood on the pavement outside Turner's Emporium, and behind the direction she was facing at her table. No male company had come. She did look around once, possibly conscious of my inquisitive eyes, but my face was buried in *The Leavenworth Echo*.

*

I'm sitting at my study desk with the plate that I've taken from its upright stand on the bookshelf. My open copy of Milton's *Paradise Lost* has offered little diversion. I'm not sure how long the plate's been here. My imagination has created something real and not illusionary. Surely imagination can only exist in the real, and not in nothingness.

If I were to show you the plate now, and report my attraction for the girl, you would probably look at me curiously, even a little sympathetically, and say, 'Yes, she's pretty,' and turn away, marvelling at my dotage, and wondering what it reveals of me. You might even confide the episode to friends in a hushed voice and with a shake of the head.

So what is her appeal? Of course her ready looks mean something, but appraising a woman by her looks alone is both superficial and demeaning. Such appraisals are a reflection of media endorsements or, on a more crude level, the topic of bar room talk and male bravado. Her attraction is more than that.

She's a lady in a non-Jane Austen unsophisticated way that projects innocence, modesty and a lack of pretentiousness. But that is not a sufficient explanation either. Perhaps it's her vulnerability, her need to be protected. I sense her dream, the great universality of dreaming, nowhere more apparent than that abstracted look on her face, and I know that whatever her dream might be, it can only be achieved with disappointments along the way.

And so I feel the need to offer her my hand, and help her from that solid wooden bench, to lift her from her two-dimensional prison on the plate, and watch her grow in healthy transmutation, to become corporeal, until from tentative beginnings, and my reassurances, we seek each others arms, a buffer from the world's slings and arrows, certainly not with passion, but with understanding and tenderness.

*

The impasse was becoming adolescent and needed to be resolved. Standing in the middle of the pavement reading the newspaper would have to eventually excite people's attention, if it hadn't done so already. What was to stop me sitting at an adjoining table and ordering coffee? That would seem to be perfectly reasonable. And so I entered the tea room, to be heartily greeted at the door by a beaming female proprietor.

I expected to find my own table, but as I was heading towards one, my plate girl smiled warmly as I passed and, without standing, motioned me to the seat opposite. It was a look of relief and obvious pleasure, but not of excitement, as though we were long-established friends habituated to regular meetings.

'The cream tea is coming,' she said gently with a hint of American accent. 'I told them to wait until my friend arrived.'

It came almost immediately. We exchanged the typical greetings and gave the usual responses. After that, I'm not sure what we spoke about, but I remember feeling the need to affirm and to reassure, though I'm not sure I knew even then what needed reassurance. It certainly wasn't 'deep and meaningful' conversation, and while there were long silences, they were not uncomfortable. It wasn't the exuberant talk of incipient lovers, gluttons for epiphany, eager to find a more rational or defensible reason for their attraction.

She was everything her plate picture foreshadowed. She ate with a delicacy that wasn't overly mannered, applying the jam and cream to the second half of her scone only when she had finished the first, and not cocking her little finger as she drank her tea. The glow of her face was enhanced by the sun that slanted through the window, blushing her cheeks and gilding her ringlets of hair the colour of honey. The hint of shyness or reserve gradually disappeared like leaves drifting from branches in the fall, and caused me to query my view of her vulnerability. She was a very attractive young woman. Perhaps my need to protect her was something less platonic, less noble.

We sat for some time after we'd finished the tea before she signalled her departure by reaching for her purse. We stood together, reached out our arms at the same time, and held each other in a brief and loose embrace.

Her face was averted but a ringlet of hair brushed my cheek. 'Thank you so much,' she said. 'I'm really doing very well,' and she left with no tears, and no plans to meet again.

*

I've returned the plate to its stand where the girl sits in her two-dimensional world, forever looking distantly over my shoulder at the rows of my books, watching over other histories. After the inspiration has been removed, I return to a plain sense of things. I have come to the end of imagination.

It may be several weeks or a few days before I stop on the way to my desk as I enter the study, either for a brief hello, or to commune with her again. I haven't given her a name. Perhaps to do so might set her apart from the generality of humankind, give her a special status beyond abstraction. I resist the temptation despite our affinity. It would have to be a name that has no other associations for me.

I've come to realise that for me she's more than an exemplar. I'm the naive idealist, the ingenuous romantic and eternal dreamer who needs someone to defend.

When I confided my feelings about the impact of the picture to a close friend, broadening its claim on me beyond the particular, by telling him that I felt this desire to protect her, not so much to intercept her inevitable suffering in realising her dream, but to comfort and reassure, he laughed good-humouredly.

'Of course it's sexual,' he said, 'no different from the welter of fantasies we men indulge.'

'But why her?' I nearly protested, before I realised that it confirmed his opinion. I know now he's right.

And yet these feelings, even with their amorous expression, embrace a far larger world of male and female, young and old, all salient with their own dreams, with their captivating looks and acts and words – the old and infirm gent relic of a dying breed who doffs his hat in passing by, the chastened child struggling to comprehend a baffling world, the disenchanted lover discovering the caprice of emotion, the ancient widows in their threadbare rooms with photos of receding pasts, the couples battling to preserve the frail nobility of their love, the young exasperated mother wheeling bawling children in the mall, the looks of resigned acceptance, uncertainty, yearning, puzzlement, pain, entreaty and grief...

I continue to be seduced by small humilities I feel poignantly, that make my heart lurch, impressions bearing all the longings of a frail yet shared humanity.